IN GOOD TIME

THE SIREN ISLAND SERIES
BOOK SEVEN

TRICIA O'MALLEY

D1603375

LOVEWRITE PUBLISHING

IN GOOD TIME
The Siren Island Series
Book Seven

Cover Design:
Damonza Book Covers
Editor:
Jena O'Connor, David Burness

"Life is inherently risky. There is only one big risk you should avoid at all costs, and that is the risk of doing nothing." – Denis Waitley

CHAPTER 1

*T*his is why he rarely drank.

Nathan shook his head as though it would clear the alcohol-induced fuzziness from his mind and slipped off his glasses to rub them on his t-shirt. Putting them back on, he squinted at the water. The light from the moon danced across the surface of the midnight blue ocean, the waves lapping gently on the sandy shoreline. He'd chosen this route home from the bar, as he liked to walk the beach when it was empty to avoid any forced conversations with strangers.

Making polite conversation with people he didn't know was high up on Nathan's list of most-hated activities. He'd rather talk to people about their thoughts on crypto-currency or whether they believed in aliens – but those topics weren't usually something he could bring up in casual conversation. Talking about the weather or what someone did for work on the island only took a conversation so far, and then it would stall out, leaving Nathan bored and uncomfortable as he searched for a topic that wouldn't make him look awkward or weird.

Which…he was. A computer science nerd, to be exact. Extra emphasis on the *nerd* portion of that description.

Nathan narrowed his eyes at the ripple on the surface of the water that had originally caught his eye. It went against the pattern of the waves, and there was typically little current in the water on this side of the island, which meant something, or someone, was in the water. Not that Nathan was going to investigate closely – he couldn't even swim – but he'd certainly call for help if it was needed. He reached in his pocket for his phone and kept his eyes trained on the disturbance in the water.

For a moment there, he'd thought he'd seen a gorgeous shimmery fin – much like a mermaid's tail – arc out of the water and splash back through the surface. Which is why he was now convinced he'd been over-served at the Island Entrepreneurs monthly cocktail gathering. Why he even went to these things, he didn't quite know – aside from his mother insisting that he leave his office and try to enjoy his time on the island.

He *did* enjoy the island when he took breaks from his work, but he liked to do so on his own. It was easier that way, and less stressful than coming up with conversational topics to fill the hours while he hiked or read by the beach. While the shyness that had been debilitating as a child had abated somewhat in his adult years, Nathan still found meeting new people to be challenging. Unless he was online, of course. There, his quiet inner confidence could shine, and he ruled his little internet kingdom under the much-revered gamer name: Laird Neptune.

Another splash of water had him moving tentatively closer to the shoreline, his eyes searching the surface of the ocean. A few sounds from the village drifted to him on the balmy night breeze, a woman's laugh, a car door slamming, and the sound of a scooter zipping down the road. But nobody else wandered this stretch of beach that ran in front of several vacation guesthouses, as most people were likely already sleeping. Nathan loved walking the beach at night, the sun's harsh rays put to bed for evening. He liked to look at the stars and dream about what life would be like in the ocean. These quiet moments by the water were where he gained inspiration for the design of his ever-popular video game series – *Poseidon's Crusade.*

The ripple appeared in the water once more, and Nathan's mouth dropped open as a head appeared. No way would someone have been able to hold their breath that long was his first thought. His second was perhaps he was dreaming, because a stunningly curvaceous and oh-so-very naked woman walked out of the water toward him. Nathan froze, his heart picking up speed, as the woman approached him, water running in rivulets down her delicious curves. Her only adornment was a net of some sorts slung over her shoulder that seemed to hold a few items. Nathan swallowed, knowing he was staring, but she was all his fantasies come to life.

Dark hair rippled over her back, and luminous large eyes studied him curiously, as he gaped at her. She was a voluptuous woman, curvy and soft and goddess-like. No thin wraith here, oh no, for this woman made Nathan clench his hands to still the urge to reach out and touch. Her breasts were large, resting softly over her rounded stomach, and the curve of her waist highlighted thick thighs and an ample bottom that Nathan had to stop himself from craning his neck to sneak a look. Realizing that he was being rude, Nathan snapped his eyes up to the woman's face and her lush lips curved in an inviting smile.

"What are you wearing on your face?" The woman asked him, and Nathan blinked, her words taking a moment to register. Her voice was low and melodious, like the gentle music of bamboo wind chimes in the wind, and Nathan had to force himself to focus.

"Um…these?" Nathan tapped his glasses.

"Yes, those. Is something wrong with your eyes?" The Goddess tilted her head, and then surprised him when she reached a hand forward to tap a finger against his lens. A drop of sea water fell from her hand to his cheek, startling him from his stupor, and he jerked backwards. "Oh, I'm sorry. Did I scare you?"

"No, it's just…I wasn't expecting you to touch the lens. Most people wouldn't, um, do that…" Nathan trailed off, uncertain how to proceed. Most people wouldn't walk naked out of the ocean after having seemingly held their breath for twenty minutes underwater either. So, there was that, too.

"Oh, right." A look of embarrassment crossed the beauty's face, and Nathan immediately felt guilty for putting it there.

"No, no, no…it's fine. Really. Yes, there's something wrong with my eyes. I wear glasses to help me with an astigmatism. Um, it just means one eye is shaped a little differently…" Nathan stuttered to a stop as the woman stepped forward so only inches separated them and looked closely into his eyes. From here, there was just enough moonlight for him to see that her eyes were a deep and stunning blue, with little flecks of gold around the center. Her nearness disconcerted him, and he'd never wanted anything more in his life than to reach out and touch her enchanting body. She was what dreams were made of – and if he was sleeping right now – he hoped to never wake up as nothing in his imagination could have crafted such a perfect woman.

"They don't look different to me," the woman said, peering through his glasses.

"Oh, it's not something you could see without…I'm sorry, what are you doing here? Were you just out for a swim? Do you need a towel?" Nathan glanced over his shoulder to scan the beach for a pile of clothes. Perhaps she was staying at one of the nearby guesthouses.

"I was out for a swim. Yes, that's what I was doing. It's a pretty night, isn't it?" The woman smiled up at him. "You're quite handsome. Would you like to spend time with me?"

Every second of every hour of every day, Nathan thought but stopped himself from saying those words out loud. His shyness kicked in, and he waited a moment to try and force out something that wouldn't make him seem like a complete fool.

"Oh, is that not something you'd like? I understand. I'll find the next person to talk to. I'm certain there's more around here…" The woman stepped a few feet back and turned to scan the beach, giving Nathan a view of her ample and glorious backside. His heart almost stopped when he thought about her going to find another man.

"No, *no*, please don't misunderstand. I'd love to spend time with you. I was just going to ask your name is all…"

"Oh, of course…" The woman turned and beamed at him, taking his breath away once more. "I'm Prin…I'm Aurora. You may call me Aurora." She tilted her head at him in almost a royal manner and the oddness of her sparked Nathan's amusement. Of course, when he finally met a woman he could be besotted with, she was likely more than a just a bit weird. But so was he.

"Hi, Aurora. That's a pretty name. My name is Nathan. It's nice to meet you, even under such odd circumstances." Nathan could have kicked himself when he saw her expression fall.

"Is it odd? Am I being odd? Oh, well, that's not what I want." Aurora nibbled her thick lower lip in concern and Nathan rushed to reassure her.

"It's not odd. I mean it's a bit odd. But I'm weird, too. It's okay, you can be as weird as you want with me. This is a no-judgement zone, okay? You're safe here." Nathan held up his hands while she studied him.

"I like you, Nathan. You're very sweet and really quite handsome. I like a man that is bigger than me. You look like you are well-fed." Aurora scanned Nathan's body and he immediately straightened and tried to suck in his stomach a bit. He lifted weights, and exercised, but his body frame ran more to stocky than six-pack surfer abs. His last girlfriend had loved cuddling with him because she'd said he'd made her feel safe and she'd called him her teddy bear. Nathan internally winced at the thought, since his ex-girlfriend had then promptly left him for one of those lean surfer dudes. She claimed it was because she wanted to travel and party more, and that he was too focused on his career. Nathan didn't blame her, but his ego had taken a bit of a blow at the time. Now, as Aurora openly ogled him, Nathan crossed his arms over his chest, hoping the move would make his muscles pop a bit.

"Yes, well, I do try to eat well. I could...um take you out to eat sometime, if you'd like that?" Nathan mentally patted himself on the back for forming a coherent sentence and asking her out as well. Two personal wins, right there.

"Take me where?" Aurora squinted and turned to scan the ocean. "To the water?"

"No, to a restaurant. For dinner. A meal. Together... like...a date," Nathan said. Embarrassment rushed through him. Had he misinterpreted what she'd said? Maybe he was being too forward.

"Oh! Yes! A date. I've heard of those. Yes, please. I'd love to do that. Can we go now?" Aurora beamed up at him and it took all of Nathan's willpower to not immediately accept.

"Well, unfortunately, no. The restaurants are closed now. It's quite late, actually. But tomorrow? I could take you somewhere for breakfast. Or lunch, if you sleep late. Or dinner, or..." Nathan trailed off in embarrassment.

"Oh, right. Of course. Breakfast sounds nice. That's the closest time, and I do think you are so handsome. Will you kiss me?" Aurora tilted her chin, so that her glorious face was lit by the moon, and Nathan knew, *he knew*, that he probably shouldn't kiss her. But he'd had enough alcohol that night to lower his inhibitions a bit, and since she'd asked...

Nathan stepped forward and, cupping her face gently

in his palms, he brushed his lips softly over hers. Once, twice, and then a third time as she leaned into him, her hands coming to his chest. Heat bloomed instantly inside him, a connection running between the two of them, and Nathan could have sworn he felt his heart stand up and cheer. When she opened her mouth in invitation, Nathan deepened the kiss, tasting the saltiness of the ocean on her tongue.

"Excuse me?"

Nathan instantly dropped his hands from Aurora's face, stepping backwards as though he was guilty of breaking the law, and turned to the voice.

"Is everything okay here?" A blond woman stood before him, a sarong wrapped loosely around her curves, and Nathan recognized her as one of the women who ran The Laughing Mermaid guesthouse. He'd helped them set up a new internet mesh network recently when they'd run into trouble and had been rewarded with one of the best homecooked meals he'd had in years.

"Hi, Mirra, right? It's Nathan. I helped you with your…"

"Oh, right. The internet. Hi, Nathan. I just wanted to check on you both as I've been looking for our guest. Glad to see you've found her." Mirra raised an eyebrow at him, but there was no judgment in her eyes, just curiosity. "Am I interrupting a…date?"

Nathan wasn't sure what kind of date would result in him being fully clothed while Aurora was stark naked and dripping wet, but he bit his tongue.

"No, we aren't on a date, yet. He's asked me to do that.

Tomorrow. We're going to eat breakfast, lunch, and dinner together," Aurora said, happiness lacing her voice.

"Is that right?" Mirra shot him a look and Nathan shrugged one shoulder.

"I, uh, did ask her on a date and gave her some options. I'd be delighted to take her out for the day, of course."

"Oh, is that not what you meant?" Aurora's brow crinkled in concern and Nathan reached out to touch her arm.

"It's whatever you would like to happen, Aurora. I'd like to see you again," Nathan promised her.

"Aurora…" Mirra seemed surprised at the name, but when Nathan turned to look, her expression was placid. "Why don't you come up with me to the guesthouse and we'll have Nathan come by tomorrow?"

"I'd like that," Aurora smiled up at Nathan once more. "I'll see you tomorrow then. Thank you for the kiss – I deeply enjoyed it. I hope we can do more kissing tomorrow."

Nathan gulped as Mirra took Aurora's hand, pulling her close and whispering in her ear.

"Tomorrow then. Not too early. Come by around ten or so?" Mirra asked, already pulling Aurora up the beach.

"Right, ten. See you then," Nathan said, his eyes caught on Aurora's glorious backside. Working up the courage, he cleared his throat. "Aurora!"

"Yes?" Aurora turned.

"I liked kissing you, too. It was intoxicating." Nathan wanted to kick himself as soon as the words were out, but Aurora's grin only widened.

"Great! I can't wait to kiss you some more tomorrow. We can do a lot of kissing. It made me feel so warm inside.

You're a much better kisser than the…" Aurora cut off her words when Mirra whispered something in her ear again, and she nodded once. "Right. Goodnight, Nathan!"

"Goodnight. Night, Mirra."

"Goodbye, Nathan. Get home safe."

"Why wouldn't he be safe?" Aurora's words trailed to him and then the two ladies were out of earshot. Nathan stood there a moment longer, making sure they returned to the guesthouse, before turning and letting out a long breath of air.

His mind whirled, trying to piece together the possibilities behind what had just happened, and he realized one thing was certain…there would be no sleep for him tonight.

CHAPTER 2

"*D*id you come alone?" Mirra asked, uncorking a bottle of wine in the kitchen. Aurora looked around, marveling at the room, and the stainless-steel box that Mirra had explained kept their food cold. Refrigerator. Aurora rolled the word around in her mind, storing it away for later, and tuned back into the conversation.

"I did. Nobody knows that I am here." Guilt slipped through Aurora, but she shoved it aside. She was a grown woman, and her mother didn't get to tell her what to do. Even if she was the queen.

"You're Princess Aurora, aren't you? I've heard tell of you…" Mirra held up a glass of wine and Aurora nodded. Moving to the table, Mirra sat and put both glasses in front of them. She'd given Aurora a pretty pink swatch of fabric to wrap around her body before she'd taken her inside the guesthouse. A place for people to sleep when they traveled. The guests paid money for it, something that Aurora had heard about from her friends who visited land. For a moment, Aurora felt overwhelmed. While she had an insatiable thirst for knowledge and was deeply excited to learn more about this world, she also didn't like feeling stupid. And right now? She felt all kinds of stupid for how she'd invited the handsome man on the shore to kiss her and then to eat three meals in a row. Mirra had hurriedly explained that wasn't the norm here, and now she wondered if Nathan had just been making fun of her when he'd agreed to kiss. It hadn't felt that way, as she was certain he'd enjoyed it, but now she couldn't be sure what to think.

"I am. From the Triste Islands. I wasn't really thinking when I left, but I knew that if I wanted a chance to experience what life was really like on land, then I needed to go elsewhere. Someplace different. Someplace I wouldn't easily be found." Aurora shrugged one shoulder and took a sip of the wine. It was fruity, with a dry undertone, and she found she liked it.

"What are you running away from?" Mirra's voice held no judgement, and Aurora took her time answering while she absorbed all the new-to-her things in the room. There was another silver box on the counter, and she desperately wanted to ask if that kept things cold as well or served another purpose. When the moment drew out, Mirra looked over her shoulder to see what Aurora was staring at. "That's a toaster. It makes bread warm and crispy."

"I have so much to learn…" Aurora blew out a breath and took another sip from her glass before clenching her hands together in front of her on the table. "Basically, all of my friends and family have been allowed to spend time on land. Now that they are trying to reach out and unify the Mer tribes around the world, it's like a whole new world has opened to our people. I keep hearing of all these wonderful adventures that everyone gets to go on, but my parents have flatly refused to allow me to explore. I understand that I'm the princess, but shouldn't that make it even more important for me to understand what life on land is like? How am I meant to rule down the road if I don't understand both worlds?"

"That's a fair point, Aurora. But I'm sure your parents are worried for you. Did you tell anyone where you were going? Or leave a note?" Mirra asked.

"No. They would just come after me then. I wanted…" Aurora ran one finger up and down the stem of the wine glass as she tried to formulate her thoughts. "I wanted something more, you understand? I've been kept so sheltered and only trained in the way of the Mer. But I know there is so much more to learn and explore. And I just have this insatiable thirst for knowledge. I've always been this way and I'm always getting in trouble for it." Aurora shrugged again. "How did you know who I was?"

"Well, my mother's fiancé, Ezra, is the one who is leading the charge to unite all the Mer. We've been helping him gather information on the various tribes around the world. I took particular interest in the ones closest to us, thinking that I might get to meet you all someday. And, well, here you are!" Mirra beamed at her. "Plus, when I saw you naked and dripping wet, I very quickly realized what was going on. When I got closer, I could sense your magick, so it was easy enough for me to get a read on the situation and help you out."

"I made a fool of myself." Aurora pushed out her bottom lip.

"No, no…please don't think that." Mirra reached across the table and squeezed her hand. "I'm certain you made every dream of Nathan's come true. I mean…just look at you. A gorgeous naked woman on the beach asking for a kiss? He'll be happy as can be. Trust me."

"He won't think I'm stupid?" Already, Aurora wanted to see him again. Not only had she enjoyed his kiss, but she liked the gleam of admiration she'd seen in his eyes.

"I don't believe so. But…there's a problem, Aurora."

"What's that?" Great, more problems to deal with and she'd been there less than an hour.

"You have to understand that humans don't *actually* believe in mermaids. They don't think we exist. They love our myths and our stories, but they don't think we are real."

"Wait…not at all?" Aurora's mouth dropped open. How was that possible? How could they deny the existence of an entire population? "I thought that is why Siren Island was so popular. Even I've heard how mermaids are celebrated here. It's why I came in this direction."

"The *myths* of mermaids are celebrated. And, yes, some humans do know and believe in us. But the majority? They don't believe. We reveal ourselves to very few people. You'll need to be careful here and protect yourself." Mirra's face held a look of concern.

"Does this go back to the days where the sailors captured our people?" Aurora's heart fell. She'd thought that going to land would be easy, but already it seemed much more complicated than she had anticipated. She'd wanted to explore, have some fun, and learn about a new place. Now, it seemed like her actions could put her and her people in jeopardy. Perhaps her parents had been right to be so strict with her. But she was almost thirty years old, and it was far past time for her to branch out, as far as she was concerned. She hadn't had a "first" in years. She'd had a first kiss, a first love, more than one lover since, and she'd flown through all her training, studies, and arts she could learn as a mermaid. Quite simply, she wanted *more*.

"Well, I'm sure you know our history. How we hid for so many years. It's just recently that we are slowly integrating with humans again. But honestly? It's a slow process. You have to be careful who you trust with your secret. It matters – and it could cost you your life. In the wrong hands? You could be exploited."

Aurora sighed and slumped in her chair.

"More rules," Aurora said. "I struggle with those."

"Many do. But these are to keep you safe. Because if you don't have your safety, then you don't really have autonomy do you?" Mirra said, finishing her glass of wine. She stood and moved back to the refrigerator. "Can I make you some food? I'm sure you have a billion questions and I'm happy to help. I can give you a space to stay here for a bit, as my mother is traveling. You can use her room. Our guesthouse is full of people, humans – that is, so we are really busy right now and I can't be with you all the time. Maybe I can help you with some of the basics if you're set on staying here and exploring. Do you...were you given the magick to stay?" Mirra turned, a question in her eyes.

"Like to stay on land?" Aurora tilted her head in question.

"Yes, there's a special ritual to be done. Our grandfather gifted it to us, which is why we've been able to stay on land as long as we have, though we return to the water quite frequently. However, if you stay out of the water too long – you'll get sick. You know that, right? Please tell me they gave you the basics?"

Aurora bit her lip and shook her head to indicate they hadn't. Her thoughts whirled – did this mean she was here on borrowed time?

"Your best bet will be to head into the water each night and change into your Mer form. It will rejuvenate you and then prolong your time on land. It's, honestly – well, *maybe* it's not even real. Maybe you'll be just fine without this supposed magick ritual." Frustrated, Mirra turned and slapped her hands on the counter. "Our grandfather, in the hopes of protecting his people, misled a lot of us. I can't help but think of several of my friends who lived as human for years before discovering their Mer bloodlines. How is that possible? Why were they fine to live on land but our people are told we'll die if we do? I just…I hate unfairness and it all feels very unfair. Like we are being kept in the dark about things we should know more about."

"So…I don't have to change each night? Or do I?" Aurora asked. Maybe she had taken on too much by running away from her home.

"I don't know. And that is truly the annoying part. So, let's just set some basic parameters to keep you safe while you have your little adventure and then we can see where the week goes, okay? We'll just take it day-by-day for now. There's a lot you don't know about humans and how they operate. Not everyone has good intentions here, so you'll need to be less trusting."

"I understand." Aurora smiled when Mirra raised an eyebrow at her. "No, really I do know. I've learned the history and understand that humans can be capable of harm."

"I suggest you be careful in what you reveal to people. Particularly Nathan if you spend time with him." Mirra pulled various food items from the fridge and began to arrange them on a plate.

"You know him? He seems nice, doesn't he? I like him. He's very handsome and I liked how he kissed me. It felt…" Aurora thought back to his lips on hers. His kiss had seemed to wake something in her, making her crave something more, and she hadn't wanted him to stop. "Really great, to be honest. Not like the Mer I've kissed. I want to kiss him again."

"I'm sure he'd be more than delighted to indulge you," Mirra said with a smile. "But just take it slow there. I only know him a little bit and he strikes me as very intelligent, kind, and a bit shy. Perhaps awkward even. Someone like you could easily overwhelm him."

"Oh really?" The thought of having that kind of power over a man excited her. Aurora was used to very confident Mer who always took charge. It would be nice to have the roles reversed a bit.

"The look on your face is a touch disturbing." Mirra laughed. "Be careful with his heart, Aurora. If he's truly a nice guy, he may bruise easily."

"Well, then, *help* me." Aurora threw up her hands. "I don't like feeling like a fool – and I will if I don't have some basic guidelines to go by here. So, am I to understand that you don't kiss and have sex right away here?"

Mirra threw her head back and laughed. She came to the table and poured more wine into Aurora's glass.

"It depends. Unfortunately, women who chose to have sex with someone they haven't known very long are often branded in an unflattering way. However, recently there has been a push for women's sexual choices to be accepted as easily as a man's are."

"How so?" Aurora thought, confusion making her furrow her brow. "Why is there judgment if people choose to be with each other?"

"There shouldn't be…but quite often men are forgiven if they have a lot of partners, but women are harshly judged. Luckily, that mentality seems to be changing a bit."

"Really? That's strange. The Mer don't make you feel bad for celebrating each other's pleasure…" Aurora bit her bottom lip, thinking it over. "Why is it such a big deal?"

"That, my dear, would take ages to unpack. Basically, what I'm saying is that it's a small island and people will talk. Particularly if you were to be with a different partner each night. I would caution you to go slow in that area until you get a better handle on how the world works here." Mirra put a platter of fruit, cheese, and bread in front of them and plopped back into her chair.

"I'm fine with that. I've always been particular about my choice of partners, but that's with the Mer. Most of them I've grown up with and are like brothers to me anyway, so it's not like I've had my taste of them all," Aurora laughed and picked up a grape. "I've had these before. My friend brought some fruit home. It was delicious."

"Yes, grapes. They are quite tasty and also used to make the wine you are drinking." Mirra gestured to her glass.

"Really? I have so much to learn," Aurora sighed.

"We'll start with some basics. Like…how to get around the island. How money works. And basic etiquette when meeting new people. How does that sound?"

"That sounds perfect." Aurora beamed at Mirra and reached over to squeeze her hand. "Thank you for taking care of me. I guess I'm lucky you found me. I'm not sure where I would have ended up without you."

"Likely in Nathan's bed, if what I saw between you was any indication…" Mirra chuckled.

"And…I still might. If I like him…" Aurora teased, and popped another grape in her mouth, enjoying the juicy sweetness. Now that she'd gotten over her embarrassment, and Mirra would teach her a few rules, she was ready to have some fun on Siren Island.

CHAPTER 3

*T*rue to form, Nathan had stayed up most of the night obsessing over his meeting with Aurora, while playing an epic battle online in his video game world. Though he'd wanted to chat with a few of his online friends about the woman he'd just met, there was something that made him hold back. She'd both confused and enchanted him, and until Nathan could spend more time with Aurora, he wasn't quite ready to share any details about her. Instead, he'd tried to commit every detail of their meeting to his memory, never wanting to forget the most exciting kiss he'd ever had in his life.

He had questions. A lot of them, actually. While the kiss had shown him that Aurora was all woman, her questions had seemed almost childlike. Now that the cloud of alcohol had cleared from his brain, he worried that perhaps he'd taken advantage of someone who might be dealing with a few issues. He couldn't be sure, perhaps she was just enthusiastic and direct, but the fact that his glasses had confused her, and she'd seemed easily excited about eating three meals in a row with him, well…it had been a highly unusual interaction. Not to mention the fact that she'd been under the water for quite some time when he'd finally watched her surface.

His eyes found a painting he'd bought in a little island shop that doubled as a café that he liked to go to for sandwiches and coffee when he was feeling a bit more social. He'd hung the painting over his computer, so his gaze could drift to it while he worked through programming issues. The acrylic painting depicted a luscious mermaid – her soft curves accented by deep shades of blues and greens as she lounged, almost languid, across the rocks with a come-hither smile on her face. Now, she reminded him of Aurora, and he hadn't been able to tear his eyes away from the painting as a silly thought danced through his head.

No, Nathan firmly reminded himself. Mermaids weren't real. That was just sleep deprivation after a night of alcohol kicking in. In all likelihood, Aurora was just an island eccentric. Nathan had learned very quickly that all kinds of people found their way to Siren Island…drifters, wanderers, artists, and retirees. Many of them didn't like to speak of their past, something Nathan could understand, and the island seemed to embrace the odd characters as part of the local charm. It was a respite from judgement of the real world, and Nathan had learned to appreciate the quirkiness of many of the people he'd met since he'd landed on Siren Island.

A beautiful island eccentric. That is all Aurora was. One whom he had a date with in…Nathan blinked at the clock and realized he was meant to be going to The

Laughing Mermaid in under an hour. Shooting out of his chair, he signed out of his video game and sent his team a harried email explaining he was going offline for the day. Unusual for him, but they'd probably be pleased he wasn't hovering over their work.

Nathan dashed from his office in the villa he'd rented by the water, and into his bathroom so he could shower. Ducking his head under the spray, he tried to come up with a plan for the day. It wasn't often that a stunning woman like Aurora took notice of him, so he needed to do something that would impress her. Money wasn't an issue for him – should he go all out? Cursing himself for letting time get away from him, as he could have been on the phone arranging something fancy, he scrubbed his hands over his face. Okay, he needed to calm his anxiety and just think for a moment.

She'd seemed both excited and uncertain last night when she'd asked about spending more time together. If he didn't want to overwhelm her, perhaps keeping it simple would be best. She knew next to nothing about him, so why would she feel comfortable going off on some fancy all-day date with him. If he wanted to learn more about her and earn her trust, he needed to take this one step at the time.

So, first things first – he'd arrange breakfast and then take the day from there.

Toweling off, Nathan threw on board shorts, a white t-shirt, and a short sleeved Hawaiian print button-down over the top. Sliding his feet into flip-flops, he moved to the kitchen to see what he had for food. A quick perusal of the contents of the fridge revealed a slew of Diet Cokes, several bags of chips, and one lonely apple. That would *not* do. Nerves began to kick in and sweat beaded his brow as he worried about what do for Aurora.

Coffee. Nathan snapped his fingers. Not only would *he* need coffee, but she would likely expect coffee as well. He could go get a takeaway breakfast for her and then see where the day would take them. Glancing at the clock, he realized he had just enough time to run to the little art shop café, and back to the Laughing Mermaid.

Thankful the shop was empty when he arrived, Nathan beamed at the lovely woman, Lola, who greeted him.

"I haven't seen you in a while," Lola said with a warm smile. The island wasn't at a loss for beautiful women, as she possessed a confidence that had often made Nathan tongue-tied in the past.

"I've been on a deadline." Nathan didn't have time to be awkward in the presence of Lola's sultry beauty this morning. "I need food for a date. A breakfast date. And coffee. Please."

"Ah, a date. That's fun, isn't it? What does she like?" Lola asked, her smile widening.

"I have no idea." Lola must have read the panic in his eyes, because she just nodded and turned away from the counter.

"I'll put together an easy breakfast selection then." In moments, the coffee grinder sounded, and Lola puttered away in the kitchen while Nathan wandered the room. The store was set up close to the water in a traditional island-style hut, with shutters thrown open to encourage the ocean breeze. Above, large palm-frond fans pushed the air around the room, and the sound of the ocean danced through the door. The store itself held an eclectic mix of art, from paintings to carvings, and Nathan always enjoyed seeing what new items had arrived since he'd last visited. When his eyes fell on a pretty bracelet made of sea glass beads with shiny abalone shells, he picked it up. For some reason, he thought Aurora would like it, and he brought it to the counter as Lola packed a brown paper bag full of food for him.

"Um, can I get this as well?" Nathan held up the bracelet.

"For your date?" Lola surmised.

"Is it too much?" Again, anxiety made him pause.

"First date?" Lola guessed, and Nathan nodded.

"I think it's a very sweet gesture. It's not an expensive or over-the-top gift and won't make her uncomfortable as being too forward. Next time, flowers are just as nice, but I'd say she'd appreciate the gesture. You can just tell her that it reminded you of the ocean and is a nice keepsake for her. That's something that can be given between friends, as well."

"Right, reminds me of the ocean. Got it," Nathan blew out a relieved breath.

"I didn't have time to cook anything for you, as you said you were in a rush, but I've packed bagels, croissants, granola, fruit, and yogurt. Plus I've added a few small jars of jam and butter. That should be enough for an easy breakfast that most people would eat. And coffee in to-go cups with creamer and sugar on the side."

"You're amazing. You've saved me," Nathan said, paying with his card and adding a generous tip.

"Let me just put the bracelet in one of our pretty mesh bags."

Nathan waited while she slid the bracelet in a rainbow-hued sparkly mesh bag and handed it over to him.

"Thank you. Truly."

"Good luck. Report back if you get a chance…I'm nosey," Lola laughed and turned to greet the next customer that came through the door.

Nathan dashed out of the door and to his Jeep where he secured the food before hopping in the driver's seat. It was another beautiful day on Siren Island. Cotton-puff clouds dotted the cerulean sky, boats cruised from the harbor, and couples walked together along the shoreline. It was peaceful here, albeit a bit slow, but Nathan didn't mind this pace of life. Cities were overwhelming for him and required too much maneuvering and focus. Here, he could navigate his life easily, and he'd just extended the lease on his villa for another year. The last year had been his most productive one yet, and both his fans and his developers were delighted with the new ideas he'd brought for his game world.

Nathan skidded the Jeep to a stop at precisely ten and he breathed a small sigh of relief. At least Aurora would know he was reliable, even if it wasn't abnormal for him to lose track of time when he was working. It was one of the reasons he worked for himself. Time seemed to become meaningless when he was lost in programming or building a new concept. Perhaps it wasn't always the healthiest to sit at his computer for hours on end – but he loved his work.

"Nathan, how nice to see you again." Mirra stood at

the door in a simple sundress that made her look like a million dollars. Again, there was no shortage of beauties on this island, Nathan thought as he offered her a smile. When he'd come to work for the ladies of The Laughing Mermaid, he'd been bowled over by both the sisters', as well as their mother's, good looks. They sure packed a punch, but now, seeing Aurora again as Mirra led him through the house and out to the back, he thought they paled in comparison to her beauty.

His mouth went dry as he drank in the full effect of Aurora in the daylight. A weaker man would have dropped to his knees, groveling before her beauty, but he was certain that would make him appear even more awkward than he was. So, while he mentally genuflected to the goddess who stood before him, Nathan just offered her a smile.

"Good morning, Aurora. You look beautiful and, um, put together this morning." Damn it, Nathan thought. Why did he have to add the *put together* part? Now he was implying that she wasn't normally put together. Heat singed his cheeks.

"Why would I not be put together? Am I missing pieces?" A worried look crossed Aurora's face and she glanced down at the simple turquoise tank dress that flowed over her opulent curves. Her hair had been braided back from her face and fell down her back in waves, and the blue of her dress only heightened the stunning color of her eyes.

"It's just a saying," Mirra interrupted.

"Oh, right," Aurora nodded, looking back up at Nathan.

"I brought breakfast, as I had promised you food," Nathan said, hoping to move past the awkward moment. He held up the bags of food. "I hope you're hungry."

"I am," Aurora assured him. "I love to eat."

"As do I," Nathan said. He turned to Mirra, sensing her concern. "Would you like to join us? There's plenty. I thought we'd just sit outside here for breakfast and talk a bit, if that suits?"

"Yes, that would be fine." A quick look of relief was replaced by a smile. "But I won't be joining you. I have new guests arriving, so I'll be handling that. Enjoy your morning." With that, Mirra disappeared with a fluttery little wave, and Nathan turned back to look down at Aurora. For a second, the absolute beauty of her stole his thoughts and he just stared dumbly while she blinked up at him.

"Is everything okay?" Aurora finally asked, twining a lock of her hair around her finger.

"I think you're the most beautiful woman I've ever seen," Nathan said, and then flushed, wanting to kick himself for not being smoother with his lines. He knew the ladies liked it when a man was confident and even a little unavailable, and here he was basically professing his love for this woman. Might as well write "Loser" on his forehead, Nathan thought with a grimace.

"And I think you're very sweet." Aurora beamed up at him and threaded her arm through his. Her touch made his senses go haywire, as though he'd stuck his finger in an electric socket, and he allowed her to lead him to a table shaded by a cheerfully striped umbrella. The cushions on the chairs matched the umbrella, and while there were other guests making use of the loungers further down the garden toward the beach, nobody else sat near the table.

Nathan tried to take the compliment that Aurora had given him, but the word *sweet* stung a bit. His last girl-friend – the one who'd taken off with the surfer – had always told him he was too sweet. She'd like edgier guys, ones who commanded a room or would stand up in a fight. That wasn't his style, at least not offline, and now the word rankled a bit.

"I wasn't sure what you'd like for food," Nathan said, as he unpacked the bag and spread the breakfast out before her. "But I got a little bit of everything. And I also brought coffee."

"I haven't had…" Aurora trailed off, biting her lip, as Nathan sat down across from her. A gull swooped lazily in over them, investigating their table, and the scent of salt water carried to him on the breeze.

"What? Tell me…" Nathan looked at her in curiosity.

"Never mind. Thank you for bringing me food."

Nathan wondered what she had been about to say, and why her expression had suddenly turned sad. His mind worked furiously, trying to come up with something for conversation, but his anxiety had kicked in now that he was actually on a date with this gorgeous woman. What could he possibly entertain her with? He didn't even know where she was from or what she liked to do for fun. Maybe he should start there.

"What's this?" Aurora interrupted his silence by holding up the bag that had the bracelet in it.

"Oh, right. I, um, saw this and thought you would like

it. It reminded me of your eyes." Shit, he'd meant to say the ocean.

"It's so pretty," Aurora exclaimed as she pulled the bracelet from the bag and held it up. The sunlight caught the beads, making them glow an ethereal blue, and she slid the bracelet onto her wrist. "Thank you for giving me a gift. I love it."

"You're welcome," Nathan said. His anxiety abated a bit and he picked up a bagel to cut it in two. "So, tell me Aurora, what brings you to the island? Have you visited here before?" *How long are you staying?* Nathan kept the last part quiet, not wanting to appear too eager.

"I wanted something more," Aurora said, turning those brilliant blue eyes on him. "I've never been here. I didn't even really know that I was coming here until I did. And now, here I am."

Nathan wasn't quite sure what to make of that, but his anxiety lessened even more. Because now, one thing was for certain – Aurora might be even more socially awkward than he was. Which, in a weird way, made him feel comfortable. Relaxing back into his chair, he grinned at her.

"I'd love to hear more about it."

CHAPTER 4

*S*he wanted to tell him everything.

But Mirra's words of caution rose into her mind, and she clamped her lips shut before reaching for a piece of fruit from the container he'd placed in front of her. Nathan's eyes were shaded behind the sunglasses he wore, something she'd learned about this morning when speaking with one of the guests at the guesthouse. After that conversation, where the woman had given her a lot of confused looks, Aurora had realized she needed to be careful with her line of questioning or she'd be viewed as abnormal. Mirra had promised her that she would give her a whole slew of books and magazines that would help her to understand day-to-day life here. But, in the meantime, Aurora would need to try to blend in better than she had managed to do thus far.

"It's really not all that interesting," Aurora said, giving her shoulder a nonchalant shrug as though people escaped their royal Mer duties and absconded to another country every day. "I just wanted a bit of a change is all."

"Where's home?" Nathan asked, taking a sip of his coffee and leaning forward. Aurora liked how he carried himself, quietly confident and focused on her. While she was used to people paying attention to her, it was because of her royal appointment – not because of who she was as a person. Nathan knew nothing about who she was, and still his attention remained fixed on her as though she was the most interesting person in the world. It was flattering, this single-minded focus he had, and she loved how he so effortlessly complimented her. She was honest enough to admit to herself that the flattery made her feel good.

"Triste Islands."

"Really? Aren't they sparsely inhabited?" Nathan scrunched his brow as he thought.

"Um, yes, quite a small population. It's why I was looking for something different. I don't get out much," Aurora said. "It's nice to be around more people."

"What do you do there?"

"Do?" Aurora tilted her head in question. "Um, swim a lot...that kind of thing." She hoped she didn't sound like a complete idiot and ripped off a corner of a croissant to shove into her mouth to stem the flow of words that wanted to bubble out.

"I guess there isn't a lot to do, is there?" Nathan asked. "That would make sense though, about how you are such a good swimmer. You must free-dive then? I felt like you were under the water for a long time last night. I was actually kind of worried – I thought someone was hurt."

"Oh, right. Yes, I like to free-dive. The water is such a lovely place to be, isn't it?" Aurora relaxed a bit, as this was an area she could comfortably speak about.

"I wouldn't know. I don't swim," Nathan said, and reached for a croissant. Aurora's mouth dropped open.

"What do you mean you don't swim? I don't understand?" Aurora gripped his forearm in shock, and his gaze dropped to her hand. Warmth zipped between them at her touch, and Aurora was reminded of how it had felt to be in his arms last night. There was something about this man that made her want to crawl into his lap and curl up, as though he would keep her safe from the worries of the world. It wasn't a feeling she was familiar with, as she'd always had the protection of the royal guards for her safety. Now that she was much more vulnerable, she was realizing that perhaps she'd taken her day-to-day safety for granted. Mirra had spoken extensively about things she'd need to pay attention to during her stay, like not accepting drinks from strangers, and Aurora felt like if Nathan was by her side she wouldn't have to worry so much.

"I don't know how. I never learned." Nathan gave her a small smile, as though he was a touch embarrassed, and she found herself patting his arm in reassurance.

"I..." Of course humans had to be taught to swim. It wasn't something that a mermaid didn't know how to do, so she'd never considered the fact, at least not all that deeply, that humans didn't share the same easy-going relationship with water that the Mer did. "Huh, interesting. Yet you live by the water. Does that mean you never go in the ocean?"

"I'll wade up to my knees. Or I sit in the sand and let the waves run up my legs." Nathan shrugged. "I know it's unusual to come to an island and not know how to swim, but I do think the water is pretty and I find it's really soothing to listen to the waves each night."

Aurora couldn't imagine a life without the ocean. It was so much a part of her that her mind couldn't seem to grasp the concept of not going into the water each day.

"Do you want to learn? I can teach you." Aurora wasn't certain how she could teach him, but she wanted him to know the same joy she had with the water.

"No, thank you."

That was it. No explanation as to why – he'd just simply declined her offer. Aurora couldn't decide if it stung a bit that he didn't want her help or if she respected him for being confident in establishing boundaries around his comfort zone. Deciding she'd go with the second feeling, mainly because she wasn't used to people telling her no, she smiled at him.

"Well, if you ever change your mind – let me know. But I'm guessing you're not from the island then? Where's home for you?"

"I'm originally from Seattle." When Aurora only tilted her head at him in question, he paused a moment to study her, before continuing. "Um, it's in Washington State. On the West Coast of the United States."

"What is it like there?" Aurora didn't want to further reveal that she'd never heard of this place. She was realizing that the best way for her to keep Nathan engaged was going to be to ask him a lot of questions about himself so that he wouldn't focus much on her story. If she did that, maybe she could get to know him well enough that she would feel comfortable trusting him with her own past. Though she already wanted to tell him about herself, Mirra had been adamant about Aurora waiting to do so. When it came down to it, Mirra had successfully navigated the world of humans as a mermaid, so Aurora needed to trust her own kind in this matter.

"It's definitely very different. It rains a lot. Like, *a lot*." Nathan laughed. "But it's a big city with a ton of different types of people who live there. The city can be moody, uplifting, and fun – it all depends. There's a pretty solid music scene there, great bookstores, and tons of good restaurants. We aren't that far away from a lot of beautiful nature options as well, so hiking, skiing, camping…all of that is available to us. And it's much colder than here. So the heat was an adjustment for me, that's for sure. As is the sun." Nathan pointed a finger toward the sky.

"That sounds really interesting," Aurora said, leaning forward. "Tell me about the bookstores? I love to learn. Are there bookstores on the island?"

"A few small ones, I think. But mainly I read on my Kindle app," Nathan said, and Aurora stared at him blankly. "Kindle? E-books?"

"I'm not sure…" Aurora shook her head, her cheeks flushing with embarrassment.

"Oh, that's fine. Not everyone is into the e-book market," Nathan rushed on, and reached in his pocket to pull out a small silver device. A phone, Aurora had learned, when Mirra had used hers earlier that day. A phone that showed a lot of pictures and text. It was a fascinating contraption, like magic in a box, and Aurora had wanted to play with it for hours, but Mirra had needed her phone for work. "See? You can download a book and read it from your phone. Like this…"

"And the words just appear?" Aurora bit her lip as she leaned over the screen that Nathan had tilted for her to see. At home, their books were much different – made of special parchment to withstand the salt water – and well, magicked as well. It was why oral storytelling was so popular with the Mer, and why Aurora was hungry for more knowledge. Luckily, her people had been taught languages at a young age, and she knew the languages of at least fifteen different countries that she likely would never even get to visit. Now, as she sat here looking into this magical contraption that held stories, Aurora realized her people had a lot to learn. In some respects, their magick would far supersede some of what humans were capable of, and in others they were lightyears behind those who live on land. It was an interesting juxtaposition, and one she wondered if her parents understood. How would the future of the Mer align with humans as their capabilities expanded?

"Yes, I suppose that wouldn't be something you've had on Triste?" Nathan asked.

"No, not really," Aurora said. It appeared the sparse human population that lived on Triste Islands was going to work in her favor. Aurora seized on the idea, as understanding dawned. A bigger island would mean more people and more access to new technologies, while some places like Triste Island would not be as advanced. That would help to explain why she didn't know many new things and maybe, just maybe, help her not seem so odd to Nathan. "Small island, remember?"

"Yeah, in fact, I wonder if you even have internet connection there. I'll have to look it up, but I was pretty sure the population of Triste was like..." Nathan looked at her in question.

This she could answer, as she'd swam close to shore for years now, as well as having her friends report back to her after their on-land excursions.

"Hundreds, maybe? Perhaps a thousand."

"That's incredible." Nathan shook his head and peered down at his phone with a laugh. "I think there's like eight hundred thousand people in Seattle alone."

Aurora's eyes widened. That sounded...insane. She couldn't imagine being so crowded. How did they even manage to maneuver around each other?

"I can't even...I can't even think about how many people that is," Aurora admitted. "It sounds busy. And crowded. Where do you all live? How do you live? I'm used to...space." Well, when it came to the ocean. Aurora could swim for hours without passing another Mer if she chose to. Some of her most peaceful times came when she would head out for long afternoon swims, with only the ocean creatures as her company, her mind set on endless daydreams of what life could be like on land.

And now? Here she was. Living it. And never in her wildest dreams had she thought it would be so confusing. Perhaps that had been naïve of her, Aurora realized. Her friends had made it sound like going to land was a big adventure where they could just play all day and learn about new things. None of them had spoken of dangerous people, new technology, or the difficulty in navigating relationships with actual humans. Perhaps it was because they'd never stayed all that long, instead darting onto land for sexy rendezvous with random men, before returning to the sea.

But this? This was a proper adventure, and Aurora needed to be smart about how she proceeded.

"It's complicated," Nathan admitted. He leaned back and looked up into the air, as he thought about his time back in his home city. "There are tons of cars, and long lines, and it takes forever to rent an apartment. People will often live with roommates to share the rent or are forced to move further from the city to afford housing. There are a lot of inconveniences to living in a big city. But some would say the same of living on a small island."

"How so?" Aurora asked, wanting to keep him talking even though she wanted to ask what rent was.

"Well, I'm sure you can imagine!" Nathan gestured with one hand as he laughed. "I mean, it can't be easy for you to get anything on island, right? Like if you need to order something from Amazon, or need supplies, or even groceries...I'm sure it takes much longer, right?"

"Right." Aurora nodded her head dutifully. What the heck was an Amazon?

"Well, people who live in the city – they can have everything they ever wanted delivered to their doorsteps. Clothes, toys, games, food – they never even have to leave their house. It's a convenient way to live. While here, if you want to order something, it can take weeks to arrive to the island. But the trade-off is a much slower way of living. And slow doesn't always mean bad. It makes you appreciate what you have a lot more, and sometimes you realize that overnight delivery of an impulse purchase doesn't end up making you feel all that happy anyway."

"Is that what people in your city want?" Aurora asked, finishing the croissant she had been mindlessly shredding on her plate. "To feel happy with delivered items?"

"Honestly?" Nathan pursed his lips. Leaning back, he crossed his arms over his chest as he thought about it. Aurora immediately liked him more. She was used to people firing off quick answers to her questions and dismissing her. Maybe it was because not everyone in the Mer world had the capacity to answer the types of questions her insatiable thirst for knowledge required, but it was nice to have someone slow down and consider their response to her question.

"Yes, I mean, there's no reason to lie about it," Aurora said, and Nathan laughed.

"Right, of course. It's just a saying…"

"Oh, I'm sorry," Aurora said softly, mentally kicking herself again.

"No, don't be. I'm beginning to understand how sheltered you've been because of your island. Which…I think is really neat. It's refreshing to be around someone who is seeing the world with fresh eyes. I like it," Nathan said.

"Really?" Aurora leaned forward and Nathan did so too, their shoulders brushing on the table. "You don't think I'm…odd?"

"I think you're perfect just the way you are, Aurora. Let me tell you something that I've learned through the years…"

Aurora stopped him by reaching up to take his sunglasses off. She wanted to see his eyes when he spoke to her. Nathan blinked several times, adjusting to the light, and she was caught on the mossy green of his eyes. They were almost hypnotic, the way they pulled her in, and she found herself wetting her lips in hopes for another kiss from him. His gaze darted down to her mouth and back up to her eyes.

"Go on..." Aurora insisted.

"Oh, um, well...I was just going to say that I've always found the people who are the outliers – the awkward ones at parties, or the colorful dressers, or the quiet people at work – those people? Well, many may see them as odd. But I think their differences makes them fascinating."

"And I'm different," Aurora confirmed.

"Oh yeah." Nathan breathed, his eyes holding hers.

"Thank you for being nice to me. I have a lot to learn here, and I'm dying to do so. Will you help me?" Aurora asked. It was as close as she could get to admitting she didn't really know how to explore this island on her own.

"I'd love nothing more," Nathan said, excitement slipping into his eyes.

"And will you kiss me again?" Aurora didn't care that Mirra had cautioned her about so openly asking for Nathan's kisses. She knew what she wanted – and there were some things she would just have to decide for herself. If she was reading Nathan right, he was more than open to enjoying a kiss with her, so what would be the harm in asking for one?

"I was hoping you'd ask..." Nathan's voice was husky with need, and then he leaned forward, capturing her lips in a gentle kiss. When she would have drawn back, not wanting Mirra to come out and lecture her, Nathan's hand came up and threaded her hair, tilting her head to deepen their kiss.

And, oh, this was what she'd been looking for her whole life! Colors seemed to explode behind her eyes as heat raced through her, pleasure curling low in her stomach. Never had a kiss woken her so, and now she wanted more. Aurora made a soft mewling sound when Nathan pulled back, breaking the kiss, and his smile at her sound of distress showcased his quiet confidence.

"Mirra's about to come outside with the new guests," Nathan said, squeezing her hand before leaning back in his chair and taking a sip of his coffee. Only now could Aurora hear the approaching voices and she understood why he'd broken the kiss.

"Will you show me some of the island today? After we finish breakfast?" Aurora asked. Maybe she could feel more relaxed if she wasn't worried about making any missteps with Mirra's guests. She'd yet to meet Mirra's sister, Jolie, but Mirra had warned her that Jolie would be more protective of her than Mirra had been. Maybe she could delay that introduction for a bit.

"I'd love to. I hadn't, uh, really planned anything for today as I wasn't sure if you'd actually want to see me, so I thought we'd just see how the day unfolds." Nathan shrugged, a hint of insecurity in his voice, and he put the sunglasses back on his face.

"Well, that's just silly. I told you that I wanted to see you again, didn't I?" Aurora said with a smile, her heart warming more for this delightful man.

"People don't always mean what they say." Nathan's

tone held a bitter note, and Aurora immediately wondered who had hurt him.

"Well, I do. And why don't you just take me somewhere that you like to go? I don't know anything about Siren Island, so it will all be fascinating for me, truly."

"In that case, let's have a wander, shall we?"

"Yes, let's." A wander, Aurora thought with glee. What a fun idea.

CHAPTER 5

"What is this place?" Aurora gaped at the track in front of them. She was already on sensory overload from her first ride in a car, and adrenaline made it feel like her body was humming with excitement.

True to his word, Nathan had taken her to explore the island in his open-air car. She'd asked why his car didn't have doors like the others she'd seen on the road, and he explained that some cars, like Jeeps, had doors that could be removed to make it a different riding experience. So, she'd used the strap to secure her body to the seat and had marveled at how fast the road had whipped by beneath the wheels of the Jeep. The speed of it, along with the breeze rushing through the car, had made her almost giddy with excitement. Now, she bounced on her toes and grabbed Nathan's arm. He'd pulled a hat on his head, one that had a brim to shade his eyes, and had offered her a similar one from a compartment in his car. Aurora had put it on her head, enjoying the shade it provided for her face and the clean soapy scent of him that clung to the fabric.

"It's land sailing." Nathan smiled down at her. He had nice even teeth, and a wide smile that lit his face when he laughed. He seemed to do everything with a single-minded focus, so when he laughed it didn't just light his face, but his whole body shook with it. When he explained something to her, he held her arm and furrowed his brow, concentrating on his explanation and making sure she understood his meaning. She wondered if he knew the intensity with which he lost himself in what he was doing and tried not to squirm at the thought of that focus on her during their lovemaking.

Because, oh yes, they *would* be enjoying each other's bodies later. Aurora had already decided that, but she did keep Mirra's caution in mind. Mirra had explained that, generally speaking, humans would go on several dates and build themselves up to making love. So, she would do the same. Aurora had learned that lovemaking could be a dance in its own right, and Mirra had explained that pleasure could be found in other ways that didn't require sex. It was such an interesting concept to her, to go slowly and take these acts in steps, and Aurora wondered if it would only serve to heighten her excitement. Already she wanted to do so many lusty things with Nathan, but she also could sense that he was trying to be respectful of her. Since she was essentially in a new land, and learning a new culture, Aurora would default to the guidelines that Mirra had explained to her. It seemed to be working, because Nathan was all but glued to her side, and she was certain that what she felt from him was attraction.

"But…they are boats. Boats on wheels?" Aurora tilted her head as she studied the little boats with big sails racing around a circle track. The winds were strong on this side of the island, and the sun shone cheerfully in a brilliant blue sky. It was hot, in a way that she wasn't used to, but the wind helped keep the temperature down a bit.

"Yes, that's exactly it. Basically, you'll sit in the cart and then use the rope to control your speed. They'll give you an explanation on how to do it. And then, well, we'll race."

"Race? A competition?" Aurora turned to him and grabbed his arm. "Really? I *love* to race."

"Oh, you're competitive, are you?"

"Yes, of course, it's what we do," Aurora said, and then forced herself to temper her explanation. "Swim races are my favorite."

There were other games and races the Mer would play, but speed races underwater were some of the easiest and most fun ways to settle a bet or decide who had to do a chore. Each year, there were more formal competitions where the strongest Mer would win a medal of sorts. Those competitions included things like distance swimming, speed racing, highest jump from the ocean's surface, longest boulder carry underwater, and so on. The Mer loved a good competition, and most nights they played variations of games that included physical or mental strength. This was right up Aurora's alley.

"Well, I'll take your word for it that swim races are fun," Nathan said.

If only he knew, Aurora thought, turning her eyes back to where the carts zipped around the track.

"So you picked a sailboat race that is out of water."
Aurora giggled. "I suppose that makes sense for someone
who can't swim."

"Hey, it levels the playing field a bit, doesn't it? What
do you say, Aurora? Want to race?"

"Absolutely." Aurora bounced up and down, and she
caught Nathan's glancing to her breasts and then quickly
looking away. Before they'd left for the day, Mirra had
pulled her aside and given her some clothing options to
change into. While some of the items were too small,
Mirra had found a soft pair of shorts in a pretty floral
pattern, and a loose white t-shirt. When she'd come out,
Nathan's mouth had dropped open and Mirra had grabbed
her arm and pulled her back to the bedroom. Apparently,
women wore bras *under* their clothes here, instead of as an
outfit, and Mirra had found a bikini top that fit Aurora's
ample breasts. She'd said it was better than the alternative,
and Aurora had just shrugged, unconcerned, until Mirra
had explained that the t-shirt was sheer and humans could
be shy with nudity. Another cultural thing for her to adapt
to, and Aurora tried not to be embarrassed for standing
naked in front of Nathan the night before. In all fairness,
she'd never been taught to hide her body or that nudity
was offensive, and Nathan hadn't appeared upset, so
Aurora resolved to not let that moment make her feel
awkward.

Aurora waited quietly while Nathan spoke to a man
who had waved to them from a small hut painted a stark
white. There, she saw Nathan pull out some paper from his
pocket and remembered about money. Mirra had put some

in the purse that she'd given Aurora, and now Aurora dug through it and pulled the bills out.

"Here, I can help," Aurora said. She held up the money and Nathan turned and glanced down at her hand.

"I'm paying," Nathan said, nudging her hand away gently.

"But I'm supposed to pay." Aurora pushed her bottom lip out. Had she misunderstood?

"I'm taking you on the date. I pay." Nathan turned back to the man.

"So, if I take you on a date, then I pay?" Aurora asked, poking Nathan in the shoulder. He grinned at her over his shoulder.

"No, then I pay, too."

"Wait, how is that fair?" Aurora demanded.

"It's not. But it makes me feel better about my manhood if I take care of the women on my dates. Yes, it's outdated and patriarchal crap, but nevertheless…I'll likely still pay," Nathan said.

Not wanting to make a fool of herself in front of the man behind the counter who was grinning at them both, Aurora just nodded her acceptance and filed that information away for later. Putting the money back in her purse, she turned and watched as the land boats came to the end of the course, slowing at the turn and angling into a little gravel lot. There, two men caught the boats and helped them slow down so the passenger could get out easily.

"Helmet," Nathan said. Aurora turned back and took the object he handed her, realizing it was what the other drivers had been wearing on their heads. Eagerly, she pulled it on only to have the bill of the other hat she still wore jam down and cover her face completely.

"Oh no," Aurora laughed, realizing how silly she must look.

"Generally speaking, you'll want to take your hat off before you put the helmet on," Nathan advised as he tipped the brim of her hat up and peered at her underneath it. Aurora narrowed her eyes at him.

"Thanks, I think I've got that figured out now."

"Just in case you hadn't." Nathan grinned.

"I look forward to beating you at the race," Aurora decided, causing Nathan to laugh. The sound sent warm tendrils through her stomach, and she resolved to try and make him laugh more often.

They followed the man out to where the other guys waited by the land boats, and Aurora stood close and studied the equipment as the man explained how to drive.

"You are the brake. If you pull the rope more tightly, you will go faster, if you let it go, you will go slower. To increase your speed as you go around the turn, pull the rope tighter and the sail will catch the wind. If you are worried you are going too fast, let the rope go loose and you will slow down. If you need help, drop the rope and wave your hands – one of us will come to you." The man held out a hand to Aurora and helped her step into her cart. She sat down, sliding her legs into a little tunnel, so she was cocooned by the sides of the boat. Taking hold of the rope, she tugged it a few times, feeling how the large sail above her would move when she did.

"But how do we get started?" Aurora turned and asked.

"We'll push you onto the course. Once your sail

catches the wind, pull your rope tight and you'll be off."
The man grabbed her cart and began to push her. Aurora
looked at Nathan, who looked ridiculous in a neon green
helmet with a black and white stripe down the middle. He
smiled widely and then narrowed his eyes as though he
was mad at her.

"You're going down," Nathan warned.

Aurora glanced down at his lap, and then brought her
eyes back to his. She smiled, and then bit her lower lip,
giving Nathan a very knowing look. When his cheeks
reddened, she figured she'd gotten in his head a bit, and
turned back to the racetrack. As far as she was concerned,
it was on the competitor to use all their advantages in order
to win.

Seconds after she'd been rolled onto the racetrack, the
heavy trade winds caught her sail and almost yanked the
rope out of her hand. Tugging on it, she jolted as the sail
went taut, and the little cart shuddered as it zipped along
the track. Aurora didn't want to lose her speed, but also,
she needed to figure out what she was doing, so she
released the rope a little bit so she could start to gauge just
how to work the sail. As she neared the corner, she pulled
the sail tight, thinking she would need more speed to make
the turn.

Instead, the cart never turned, and she barreled right
into the huge bales of hay that lined the track. She'd barely
had a chance to scream, so shocked was she by the colli-
sion, that she just sat there blinking at the little tufts of hay
that fluttered down around her.

"Aurora!" Nathan shouted, the sound of his feet

pounding on the racetrack reaching her. "Oh no, honey, are you okay? Are you hurt?"

Nathan crouched at the side of the cart, running his hands over her body, warmth following his touch. Stunned, Aurora blinked at him.

"It didn't turn," Aurora complained.

"What didn't turn? The steering wheel? Is it broken?" Nathan reached to the handlebars in front of her and twisted it experimentally.

Aurora narrowed her eyes at the handlebars. So that was what the man had meant when he explained about steering. She should have asked a few more questions, it seemed. Perhaps there was more to driving than she had realized.

"You're not hurt?" Nathan asked again. He reached up to cup her chin, turning her face toward his, concern in his eyes.

"No, I'm fine. Just shocked really. I didn't steer," Aurora admitted, feeling foolish, but willing enough to admit her mistake.

"You didn't steer?" Nathan asked, a quizzical expression on his face. The other men reached the cart and surrounded them.

"What happened?" The man at the counter asked.

"I didn't steer. I didn't...I...I don't know," Aurora looked up, hoping he wouldn't be mad at her. "I hope I didn't destroy your boat."

"Nah, it's fine. These things are pretty sturdy. Let's roll you back out. Do you want to keep going?" The man asked her.

Aurora's competitive spirit rose, and she took a deep breath.

"Turn the bars hard in the direction I want to go in?" Aurora clarified, putting her hands on the steering bar and testing it out. She could feel the wheels shift under the boat when she turned the bar, and it all clicked for her. Well, she'd just properly made a fool of herself, hadn't she? "I guess I got so caught up in going fast, I completely forgot to steer!" Aurora injected a note of excitement in her voice, hoping to cover the fact that she'd never actually driven before, and smiled brightly at the men. Her act seemed to do the trick, and they all nodded.

"It happens more often than you'd think." The man from the counter pulled her cart backwards and aligned her next to Nathan's. Aurora waited while he slid back into his cart and got himself situated before turning to her.

"You're sure you're fine?" Nathan asked.

"More than fine. I'm ready to go down," Aurora promised him, trying out his phrase from before. An odd look crossed his face, and then he smiled.

"Game on."

CHAPTER 6

"*J* won," Aurora argued, grabbing Nathan's hand and tugging him down the beach. The race had been close, both of their carts careening over the finish line within inches of each other, but the men at the track had declared her the winner.

"I'm not so sure about that. They were only looking from your angle. From mine, it was pretty clear that I was in front," Nathan said, guiding her toward a table situated under the shade of a palm tree.

"Not even close! I was very much the winner. I was ahead of you," Aurora argued, laughing up at him. "Don't tell me you are one of those men who can't lose."

"I am happy to admit to losing – when I *actually* lose," Nathan said, but she could see the teasing light in his eyes.

"I guess we'll have to go again, and I will beat you once more," Aurora shrugged. A colorful little house on wheels caught her attention, and she studied the line of people that stood before it. The ones who walked away held something in their hands that they then licked. "What's that?"

"That? An ice cream food truck. Would you like some? I'll get us a cone."

Aurora was too proud to ask what a cone was, but it seemed like it was a popular treat with people. And, since she was determined to learn about the human world, she wanted a chance to actually use money to pay for something.

"It costs money?" Aurora asked, just to be sure.

"Yes, it does." Nathan's lips quirked, as though the thought of a free cone was amusing, but he didn't make fun of her.

"I will go get us some."

"I can…" Aurora turned at his words and held up a hand to stop him.

"Save our seat, please. I would like to pay for the cone," Aurora said. She gave him a look that brooked no disagreement and he plopped back onto the bench and kicked his legs out, crossing his arms behind his head.

"Fine, I'll just relax here while a beautiful woman buys me ice cream."

Happy that he was letting her go on her own, as she'd be able to hide any miscommunications she encountered, Aurora approached the food truck and studied what people were doing. It seemed they waited in line, and then ordered from the words listed on the side of the truck. A sweet smell drifted to her from the open window, where a woman with a cheerful smile and a net on her head, greeted her. Aurora wanted to ask what the purpose of a net on her hair was but didn't want to be awkward.

"Hi ya, what can I get for you?" The woman waited as Aurora glanced at the words once more. She hadn't thought there would be options to choose from, and now she wasn't sure what Nathan would like. Aurora worried her bottom lip as she thought it over.

"A cone please," Aurora said, still uncertain how to proceed.

"Waffle or plain?" The woman asked.

"Waffle," Aurora said just because the word felt funny to say.

"How many scoops?"

"Um, two?" Aurora asked, since there were two of them.

"And what flavors?"

Aurora dropped her eyes to the flavor list. There were a lot of choices, and she didn't know what most of them were.

"Um, Snickers and Mint Chocolate Chip?" Aurora decided at random, noting the line behind her was growing.

"That'll be three."

Aurora stared at the woman blankly before realizing she was talking about money. Her face flushed and she dug in her purse and blindly handed the bills over to the woman. The woman glance at the wad, and then slowly peeled off one bill, before handing the rest back to her.

"Let me get you your change."

Aurora didn't say anything, terrified she'd do something else wrong, and then held out her hand when the woman passed back several more bills which she immediately shoved in her purse without looking.

"Here ya go…"

Aurora accepted the food items, staring at it for a moment before realizing she was holding the line up. Two large scoops, one brown and one green, were already dripping in a golden cakey cone. She really had no idea what to expect with this, but since it seemed to be falling apart on her, Aurora raced back to the table.

"Here." Aurora shoved the cone at Nathan, worried she was going to break it. Nathan cocked his head at her, that furrow in his brow appearing once more, and accepted the cone.

"Where's yours?" Nathan asked.

"Oh. I just…" Aurora realized it must be customary for each person to get a cone, as she glanced around and saw that most people who had left the line carried their own cone. "I thought we could share."

"Even better," Nathan said, patting the bench beside him. Aurora straddled it, leaning into him, relieved the ordeal of ordering and paying with money was over. Hopefully she hadn't screwed up the flavors too badly. "What did you choose?"

"Snickers and a mint something?" Aurora shrugged and then winced when he laughed. "Bad choices?"

"Interesting. But I'm sure it will be good. Here, taste." Nathan held the cone out and Aurora leaned in, swiping her tongue across the startlingly cool ice cream while keeping her eyes on Nathan to catch his reaction. Her intention in watching him had been to see if she was doing it wrong, but the way his eyes heated at her actions suggested just the opposite.

He found her attractive.

Perhaps there was a way to distract him while she enjoyed her first ice cream experience, Aurora thought, and repeated the action, slowly, her eyes holding his. Looking up, she licked her lips and gave a soft little sigh of appreciation.

"*That* is delicious." It was, at that, and she could see why there was such a growing line for the icy treat.

"It is," Nathan gulped.

"You haven't tasted any yet," Aurora pointed out with a throaty chuckle. "Here, let me help."

Leaning over, Aurora took a small bite of the green one, enjoying the fresh and sweet flavor, and then surprised him with a kiss. His lips opened automatically, and a tingle shot through Aurora when his tongue found hers, tasting the sweetness. The moment hung suspended, the coldness of the ice cream contrasting with the heat of their mouths, desire warming through her. A child's shout startled her from the kiss, and Nathan drew back, his gaze darting to the family sitting nearby. A faint hint of pink touched his cheeks, and she realized that she had made him feel uncomfortable.

"I'm sorry," Aurora said, leaning back. Looking around, she realized just how busy the area around them was. There were at least ten tables, all clustered under the shade of the palm trees, and then rows of loungers in the sun along the sand. The sun sparkled over the turquoise waters, and people in bathing suits splashed in the shallows.

"No, don't be," Nathan grabbed her hand and squeezed it. "Hey, Aurora, look at me."

Aurora turned, her lips clamped in a tight line, and met his gaze.

"It's not you, it's me. I…I struggle with being shy sometimes. Well, more than sometimes. I'm…I can be awkward in social situations. I have been my whole life." The pink on his cheeks deepened as he spoke, and Aurora felt bad for making him feel this way. She should have thought more carefully about her surroundings or what might be acceptable in public.

"Is it bad to kiss in public? Or around children?" Aurora asked before she could stop herself. Now, it was her turn to feel embarrassment because that was a question she should be asking Mirra, not Nathan who would only think she was strange.

"No, not at all. That was a very nice kiss. I'm just… I'm just weird, I guess. I've always dealt with this. I enjoy your kisses, and I don't want you to feel like you can't do that with me," Nathan said, running a finger across her palm.

"I like kissing you, too." Aurora looked down at where his hand tapped a beat on her palm, and then back up at him. "Why are you shy?"

"Oh, well, that's a loaded question, isn't it? Let me think where to begin…" Nathan blew out a breath and pulled his hand away, tugging at the brim of his hat. "I guess…well, I grew up with a single mom. And she worked a lot, which meant I had to go into day care a lot. I was also on my own for much of the time when I was older…after school and such. My mom's great, by the way. The best. But, unfortunately, because it was just her – she had to make ends meet. Which meant I quite often had to go sit awkwardly at various summer camps or day care programs that, well, let's just say they did the bare minimum."

Aurora just nodded, taking another bite of the delicious cone, and gestured for him to go on. Nathan paused, leaning over so he could take his own taste of the cone, and settled back into the story.

"When I was little, I struggled with speaking. It was like I knew what I wanted to say, but I couldn't get the words out. And kids can be mean to each other. After screwing up what I meant to say quite a few times, I was labeled as dumb by the other kids, and they picked on me. I *wasn't* stupid, but I couldn't get my thoughts together fast enough. Because of that, I became painfully shy. It was easier for me to be quiet than it was for me to try and speak up for myself."

"I'm sorry, Nathan. I'm so sorry you weren't supported," Aurora said, holding the ice cream up so he could have another taste. She didn't fully understand everything he was talking about, but she could comprehend the main elements of what he was saying. Later on, she'd ask Mirra what a day care and a camp was, but it sounded like a place to put children when they had no family around. It was such a departure from the mermaid world, where children were revered and the whole village looked after them, that Aurora wasn't sure how to relate to him. Instead, she just listened without judgement, wanting to know this man better.

"I think it's why I loved reading so much, and then when I discovered the online world of gaming...where I could just disappear for hours and be a different person, well, it opened a whole new world for me."

Aurora felt desperately out of her element now, with no idea of what he referred except the reference to games. That, she could understand. She wanted to support him, but not feel stupid, so she focused on what she could glean from the conversation.

"And now? You seem to speak just fine," Aurora said.

"Yes, I've since mastered the art of speaking," Nathan laughed. "It took a long time, but I got better and no longer experience those same blocks. But the shyness? Yeah, that kind of still rears its ugly head sometimes. It's just…a hard thing to break out of. But I don't want you to think you're doing something wrong if I ever get shy. It's just a *me* thing – not a *you* thing. Understand?"

"I think so," Aurora said. "And, for what it's worth, I think you're pretty great, Nathan. The man who came from the child is an honorable one and, for being someone who struggles with being shy, you certainly put yourself out there to tell me that. Which means you also are comfortable with being vulnerable to someone. I think that speaks pretty highly of you," Aurora said, hoping he would hear her admiration in her words.

"Ah, well, thanks," Nathan said, ducking his head, and Aurora had an idea.

"Okay, tell me – what's one thing you've always wanted to do but couldn't because of your shyness? Maybe we could try it together."

"Dance," Nathan said automatically, and Aurora drew back, surprised at his answer.

"Dancing. Really? You don't like to dance?" Aurora

loved to dance, and mermaids were naturally good with moving their body to rhythm.

"Yes, it puts all of the ultimate awkwardness together. Trying to stay with the beat of the music. People watching you. Stepping on the girl's toes. Making a fool of yourself. What if you have bad breath? Nope, it's too much. That's me heading for a panic attack," Nathan assured her.

"Well, then, I think we should conquer this fear. Together. Tonight. Can we dance here?" Aurora asked, eager to help.

"You want to go dancing with me? Tonight?" Nathan's face paled.

"Yes, I do. Plus you owe me another meal, right?"

"Well, two, technically. We haven't had lunch." Nathan sighed and pinched his nose.

"This is lunch." Aurora held up the cone that now had ice cream running in rivulets down her arm.

"Oh, you're just a mess," Nathan laughed. "Fine, Aurora. Dinner and dancing it is. But I may need a drink to loosen me up. And you're going to have to lead. Don't pretend you haven't been warned."

"I love to dance. This is going to be great – I promise."

CHAPTER 7

a dark-haired beauty greeted Aurora when Nathan dropped her off at the Laughing Mermaid with a promise to return in time for dinner. It would give her an opportunity to change clothes and ask Mirra all the questions she'd stored up during her time with Nathan exploring the island. It had been an incredible day, and Aurora was buzzing with excitement over all of the new things she'd learned.

"You must be Aurora? I'm Jolie, Mirra's more annoying twin sister," Jolie said, an assessing gleam in her eyes. Jolie was dark to Mirra's light, but Aurora could easily see the family resemblance between the two sisters.

"It's nice to meet you, Jolie. Thank you for letting me stay here," Aurora said. Jolie nodded once and motioned for her to come to the kitchen. Once there, Jolie slid the door closed behind them and then turned, crossing her arms over her chest.

"Yes?" Aurora wasn't easily intimidated by other women, particularly because of the fact she'd been raised to handle royal duties, so she just raised her chin and met Jolie's inquiring stare.

"What are your plans while you're here?" Jolie asked.

"I don't have any plans. Well, tonight I do. But otherwise, I'm taking it day by day while I explore. I'm here to learn, Jolie. Not to be a threat to you or yours…" Aurora said.

"You may not think you're a threat, but you could cause considerable problems for us by being here. If you're careless, that is…" Jolie narrowed her eyes.

"I don't see how I could cause problems for you. Particularly if I'm not spending time with you," Aurora said. Which she immediately decided she didn't want to do if this woman was going to be abrasive.

"Ah, well, let me elaborate. You see…you may think that you're just here on a little adventure? But your words, your actions, and how you handle yourself? Well, you can leave quite a mess behind for us to clean up when you go. And you will have to go – right? You're the princess. There's no way you can stay here, at least not long term. So, just keep that in mind when you're out using Siren Island as your little playground…there are other mermaids who live here – in secret – and need to keep those secrets protected."

"You named your guesthouse The Laughing Mermaid. I can hardly see how you are being secretive?" Aurora countered. She knew that Jolie was likely making good points, but her directness was annoying.

"Really?" Jolie drew the word out and rolled her eyes. "It's called Siren Island. We literally celebrate mermaid myths here. There are mermaids everywhere. It's part of the culture."

"So why would it be a problem for people to think there are *actual* mermaids here?" Aurora shot back. Annoyance rippled through her. She'd been in such a good mood when she'd returned, and now this cantankerous woman was stealing her glow.

"Because humans like the *idea* of mermaids. They want to have something fun to believe in. But most of them can't handle the magick we have. They won't be able to explain it with science and so they'll refuse to believe. We'll go from an idea that they find fun and charming to being hunted and exploited. It's dangerous, and you'll not help us by being careless with your time here."

"Jolie," Mirra said from the doorway. She'd just slid the door open a few inches and had caught the last of her sister's words. "Be kind. Aurora's new here."

"This *is* me being kind." Jolie poked her finger in the air. "*This* is me saving her life. And our lives. She has to realize that this isn't just some spring break for her, where she can party and then leave our lives devastated behind her when mommy and daddy come calling for her."

Aurora winced at the thought of her parents showing up to take her home. She'd go with them, she always did, and the thought that she had no autonomy over her choices rankled. She looked to Mirra in question.

"Spring break is a notorious time for younger people to travel with friends and party and make bad decisions," Mirra explained. She walked into the kitchen and slid the door closed behind her. "And Jolie does have a point, though I do wish she'd learn a touch more delicacy in her delivery."

"Well, then I wouldn't be me, now, would I?" Jolie said, shooting her sister a saccharine smile.

Though Aurora wanted to snap back and put Jolie in her place, she paused and thought through the other mermaid's words. The truth was, she didn't really know this world, not yet, and she needed help here. Even if it came in the form of a very prickly mermaid who didn't seem to particularly care for Aurora.

"I understand what you are saying. In fact, I came home with some more questions so that I can be sure to not make a fool of myself," Aurora said.

"Good, then at least you have a modicum of intelligence," Jolie said and gestured to the table for Aurora to sit. "Let's hear the questions and we'll work on some more guidelines for you."

Aurora sat, largely because she knew that Jolie was right, even though she did feel like she was being scolded for doing something wrong. However, she'd promised herself when she came here that she was going to learn, and this would mean she'd have to be willing to understand what life was like here.

"Nathan is coming back in an hour. We're going for dinner and then we are going to try dancing together," Aurora said. She looked to Mirra. "I was hoping maybe I could borrow that turquoise dress again as maybe this outfit isn't nice enough for dancing? Or is it? I'm not sure what will be proper attire here and I want to make sure I fit in."

"A makeover?" A gleam came into Jolie's eyes.

"She loves a makeover," Mirra said, and chuckled. "Quickest way to our Jolie's heart. A makeover and the promise of a good date story."

"Is a makeover..." Aurora looked between the two women.

"It's basically where you give someone new fashions to wear so they look extra nice or different than they had before," Jolie explained, leaning forward and rubbing her hands together excitedly. "It's like playing dress-up with real life dolls."

"Sure, well, then yes – let's do a makeover. And I have a lot of questions about things that I learned today. Like, what are brakes?"

Both sisters' mouths dropped open.

"Did you drive a car? Please tell me you didn't drive a car. You need special classes to do that. You can kill someone. Even yourself." Mirra held a hand to her mouth.

"No, not a car. The landsailing. With the little boats on the racetrack? They kept saying I should brake, but I was too embarrassed to ask what that means."

"Oh thank the goddess," Jolie breathed. "Brakes are a mechanism that slows moving vehicles down. You'll find them on everything from bicycles to cars. They are an important safety feature in transportation."

"Ah, yes, that would make sense then," Aurora nodded her head.

"Come, let's go dig through our closets and start the makeover. We'll discuss rules as well."

Ten minutes later, Aurora found herself standing in a small tile enclosure, and she squealed when a stream of water burst from a silver pipe in the wall.

"Oh, right," Jolie said. She let out a long peal of laughter. "This is a shower. It's how we clean ourselves here when we don't go in the ocean."

Aurora eyed the stream of water suspiciously, having huddled back against the wall. Now, she lifted a leg and was delighted to find the water to be warm.

"This is soothing," Aurora said.

"Just don't wash your hair though, it will take too long to dry." Jolie stepped behind her and piled Aurora's hair in a knot on her head and clipped it. "There. Soap is here. You take the bar and run it over your body, then rinse it off with the water. When you spend time on land, your body will sweat and make different scents than when underwater. Humans don't generally find those scents pleasing, so they clean their bodies with this."

"Baths, right? I've read about this…" Aurora was amused by the whole process, and she lathered up with the little bar of soap that held a delectable fresh scent.

"Yes, baths are like a small pool though, whereas showers are more like rainfall," Jolie's voice carried to her from the other room where she'd pulled out piles of clothes. "There is a towel to dry yourself once you are done."

While Aurora wanted to linger in the warm rainfall shower, she knew that her time was limited, and that Jolie wished to speak further with her. Mirra had left to attend to some guest needs with a quick whisper of apology to Aurora for stranding her with Jolie. Now that Aurora understood Jolie a bit better, she didn't find her as off-putting. The woman was protecting her own. Aurora could understand those motivations.

"So, a few rules," Jolie said when Aurora came out wrapped in a soft fluffy towel. "Alcohol affects us differently, but it can still make us loopy. Which means it can lower your inhibitions or make you talk too much. Wine, liquor, beer, cocktails…all of it. Go slowly when you drink. They are tasty, but you want to keep your head on your shoulders."

"Wine is the grape drink that Mirra served?"

"Yes, correct." Jolie pursed her lips as she dug through the mound of fabrics on the bed. Holding up a green dress to Aurora, she shook her head and tossed it aside. "It's very common for people to go out for drinks as humans enjoy how it relaxes them. But alcohol can also make people loud, mean, or aggressive if used in excess. For some? It makes them very happy. For others – it's not a good thing. You'll just want to monitor your usage as well as those around you."

"I will. I promise. Because if I drink a lot, I may tell people about the mermaids," Aurora surmised.

"That's right. And, either people will think you're crazy and make fun of you, or you'll reveal too much and put us in danger. When, or if, you choose to tell someone about who you really are…" Jolie turned and met her eyes, her face drawn in serious lines. "Well, that should be a choice that is made freely and when you are comfortable with the person you are speaking to. We all have people we have confided in on island."

"You've told humans about you?" Aurora raised an eyebrow. Here she was getting lectured, and Jolie was running around telling people about mermaids.

"A very, and I mean very, select few. Namely, our

loves and anyone else that is strictly need-to-know. I can count on both hands the amount of people who know about us on island." Jolie held up both hands to demonstrate how small the number was.

"Ah, yes. I suppose your partners should know who you really are, otherwise it isn't really a partnership, is it?" Aurora pursed her lips as she thought it over.

"No, it's not. But it's also not an easy conversation to have with a human. They have to see to believe. So, if that is the way things go with you...I suggest you give it time before you share that side of yourself. Particularly since you are already dating, and you've been here less than a day."

"I like him." Aurora bit her lip as Jolie held a purple swathe of fabric to her chest. "He's...he seems like a really good man."

"I think he might be. I don't know him well, but he's always been very respectful when I've met him. Quiet. But I've never gotten any bad vibes from Nathan. I can't give you any advice on whether it would be smart to share more with him or not. At some point, you'll have to decide if you just want to have fun with Nathan or if you want something serious. If it is just for fun? Well, enjoy. Have fun, relax, and play. But keep your secrets close, then, understood?"

"Is that common here? To have fun and play without revealing too much of yourself?" Aurora asked. In the Mer world, they all knew a lot about each other, having grown up in the same village. There wasn't much new to discover about a person once they'd come of age.

"Yes, it's quite common. It's harder to make real

connections where you feel comfortable speaking more deeply with people. It's why dating is difficult, but also exciting in the human world," Jolie said. She paused and threw her head back with a laugh. "Oh, wow, I used to have so much fun with them all. I would flit from man to man, and never once did I tell them who I really was. And, for the most part, they enjoyed it as much as I did. Men don't like to be tied down here. Well, some men don't. Mine does. And I'm lucky to have found him. When I knew he was the one, well, then he was safe for me to share my secret with. And he'll protect me and my family to the end. That's what really matters."

"He sounds great." Aurora pictured some hulking warrior to be Jolie's partner.

"He is. And totally opposite of me," Jolie laughed. "Ted is a professor, and he's studious, quiet, and I completely overwhelmed him when we first met."

"Really?" Aurora laughed as well. "I wasn't picturing that for you."

"Nobody does. It's great," Jolie said. "Here, I think this is what I want you to wear. You said dancing, right?"

"Yes, dinner and dancing. And drinks, but I'll be smart," Aurora promised. She looked at the silky purple dress in Jolie's hands. "That's a pretty color."

"I think the purple will pop the underlying green in those gorgeous eyes of yours. Go on, try it on."

Aurora dropped the towel and pulled the silk over her head, neither mermaid thinking twice about the nudity she displayed. The silk slid over her skin, the dress hugging her curves nicely, and Aurora grinned down at her body.

"It feels nice."

"It looks nice as well." Jolie pointed to the mirror. "Look...you're going to make Nathan swallow his tongue when he sees you."

"Oh no, I hope he doesn't do that..." Aurora said, crossing to the reflective pane of glass. Jolie's soft chuckle followed her.

"It's just a phrase for being shocked...in a good way."

"This is really pretty," Aurora said as she studied herself. The purple silk clung to her hips, flowing over her rounded stomach and bottom, and the neck draped in a way that showcased her breasts.

"It is. The cowl neck of the dress means you won't have to wear a bra, and the silk moves with your body. You're larger than me, so your body fills this dress out in a very appealing way."

"Thank you, I think this will be perfect," Aurora said.

"Now, let me do your hair and we'll talk about some things for you to expect when you're out. Like what a waitress is..."

CHAPTER 8

*N*athan stopped mid-stride, his hand paused in the air to ring the bell, when Aurora appeared in the doorway. All coherent thought left his brain and he stared at her blankly, stunned at her appearance.

Sure, he'd seen her naked the night before. A sight which was seared into his memories and would be cherished until the end of time. But this? This was something different altogether. She was sultry, and sexy, and hot, and stunning...and...the words just crammed together in his brain as desire flooded his body.

Aurora was a goddess, through and through, and he – a mere mortal – was not worthy to kiss her feet.

"Nathan?" Aurora tilted her head at him in question.

"I..." Nathan pointed to his mouth, hoping she'd remember his earlier conversation about his shyness.

"See? I told you he'd swallow his tongue," Jolie said, peeking over Aurora's shoulder. "Hi, Nathan. Doesn't Aurora look good? I'll take some of the credit for the makeover, but the rest is all hers."

"You look...incredible." Nathan finally found his words, hesitating before taking a step forward. He was scared to touch her, worried that he'd muss up her beautiful appearance. Never in his life had he seen such a stunning woman, and he was saying that with Jolie and Mirra, the two known island beauties, standing behind Aurora. The dress she'd chosen clung to every one of her delectable curves, and she didn't shy away from putting her softly rounded body on display. He liked that about her – that she was comfortable in her body – though it was large by society's standards. For him, she was perfect. He wanted to caress every inch of her soft body, her curves a playground for his hands, her lips for his taste alone. Her eyes looked darker, smudged with some smokey makeup, and her hair had been twisted back so that it flowed over her shoulders. She smiled up at him, and Nathan thought he might just be the luckiest man alive.

"Thank you. You look very handsome as well," Aurora said.

"I think I've died and gone to heaven," Nathan rushed out. "There's no way that you can be real."

A hint of...something...slipped through Aurora's eyes and Nathan instantly worried that he'd said the wrong thing.

"I'm real," Aurora promised, pressing her lips together.

"Where are you taking Aurora tonight?" Mirra interjected, drawing Nathan's gaze away from Aurora.

"Um, to Azure for dinner and then out to La Cantina for dancing."

"Oh, that's a perfect evening. It's salsa night tonight at La Cantina. You'll have fun," Jolie promised. "Just follow the other dancers…it's all in the hips." Jolie did a little swivel of her hips, and Aurora instantly copied her.

Nathan's mouth went dry as he watched the silk ripple over Aurora's body. He wasn't sure how he'd make it through the night without embarrassing himself. His need to kiss her, touch her, almost overwhelmed him as he helped her to the car. He kept his hand light at her back as he helped her into her seat, and it felt like her skin burned through the silk at his touch. Swallowing, he paused as she strapped herself into the seat and then looked at him, a question in her eyes.

"I…" Nathan gulped, and then leaned forward, cupping her chin with his hand. Leaning forward, he brushed a kiss over her lips, nuzzling close and inhaling her fresh scent. Desire warmed, and something more, as their foreheads met, and they shared the softest of kisses. It took everything in his power to pull back, but she deserved more than him just trying to take her home with him. Not that he was smooth enough to pull off such a maneuver, Nathan thought to himself as he smiled at Aurora. But also because she deserved to be wined and dined, and…danced with. The thought of dancing made his stomach twist.

"I liked that," Aurora said, her lips curving in a soft smile.

"I did too. You take my breath away, Aurora. I'm honored to have you on my arm tonight," Nathan said. There, that was nice. He rounded the front of the Jeep and soon they were cruising toward town. Nathan pulled the Jeep from the main road when they drew close to the village and found a parking spot in a little dirt lot.

"I like to park here because I can leave the car overnight if need be," Nathan explained when Aurora looked around at the parking lot.

"Why would you leave your car overnight?" Aurora asked.

"Oh, well, if I have drinks tonight – which I think I will because of, you know, my sheer terror at dancing…it's not safe for me to drive," Nathan explained. He wondered if Triste Island even had any drinking and driving laws or if it was too small to be worried about things like that.

"You don't have to dance with me if it's too scary," Aurora said as he helped her from the car. Nathan kept her hand in his, tugging gently in the direction of the street that wound along the water, and walked toward the restaurant. It was a balmy evening, with a light ocean breeze cutting the heat, and shifting the leaves of the palm trees that dotted the street. Houses and restaurants clustered together in a colorful row, and Nathan automatically nodded to a few men who sat on the front porch of a house they passed. It was common to greet people, even if you didn't know them, and Nathan had found that this cultural tradition helped with his shyness. One of the men gave him a thumbs-up, with a nod to Aurora, and Nathan bit back a grin. Though it did make him stand a bit taller, having someone like Aurora by his side.

By the time they'd been seated at an oceanfront table at the restaurant, Nathan was certain of one thing – he wanted to spend as much time as he could with this incredible woman. He'd never been around someone who seemed so obviously interested and enriched by the world around her. Aurora asked constant questions, engaged with everyone they spoke to, and seemed to be drinking in her surroundings. It was as though living on a small island had sheltered her in a way that made every experience new and exciting for her. It was refreshing to watch, and Nathan realized he could probably learn something from her attitude. Instead of looking at socializing as a trial to overcome, perhaps he needed to think of it as an adventure and a learning opportunity. It might help to scale the wall of some of the social anxieties that he still carried.

"I don't want to eat fish," Aurora said, anguish crossing her face as she studied the menu. Nathan's heart fell. He'd forgotten to ask if she was a vegetarian, and now he was likely upsetting her with his restaurant choice. He could kick himself.

"Then don't. Let's see..." Nathan scanned the menu. "You could start with the bruschetta, and then the squash risotto or the roasted vegetable pasta sounds nice."

"No fish?" Aurora crinkled her nose at the menu.

"Nope, those are vegetables only."

"Yes, then please, if you can order a vegetable only menu for me?" Aurora asked.

"How hungry are you?" Nathan asked.

"I love to eat," Aurora smiled. "I want to try everything."

Nathan found this attitude refreshing, as his last girlfriend had counted calories like it was her religion.

"In that case...let's try a little bit of it all then, shall we?" Nathan turned the menu over and pointed to the Chef's selection. "See here? They have a tapas menu, and we can just pick the vegetarian one and they'll bring a sampling of dishes."

"Oh, good." Relief flashed across Aurora's face, and Nathan wondered once more if she had some of the same anxieties that he did in social situations. For a seemingly confident woman, there were some moments where an almost child-like vulnerability revealed itself. The combination made him admire her and want to protect her at the same time. Aurora was raising all sorts of instincts in him with the first being...he wanted her. Just her.

To be his.

It was too soon for that, Nathan chided himself. It hadn't even been a full day since this woman had walked into his life. He needed to pace himself, or she'd walk right on out of it.

"Have you ever been in love before?" Nathan blurted out, after the waiter had delivered a beer for him and a glass of red wine for her. Immediately, he felt stupid. This was not the type of question to ask on a first date. He knew this because his cousin had made him watch one of those reality dating shows with him back home when he'd been helping with a computer issue. At the time, he'd squinted at the screen when his cousin had thrown up her hands and shook her head in disgust.

"What's wrong with asking about the past?" Nathan had asked her.

"Because, silly. This is like the first date. If you start asking about being in love, and, even worse, if you want to get married and have kids – well, it's just annoying. Too much, too fast, you know? Take it easy. See if there's some chemistry there first before you start digging into all the dirt from the past." His cousin had rolled her eyes.

Nathan disagreed with his cousin, but now her words rose in his head. Hopefully, Aurora wouldn't be annoyed by his question. It was just logical, he thought, to see where a person was, emotionally, when it came to dating. What if Aurora had just left a passionate relationship where she'd been madly in love with someone? It would be a horrible time for him to fall for her. At the very least, he'd be able to manage his expectations. Nathan was a big believer in understanding the parameters of a situation.

"Hmm," Aurora said. She leaned back, her curves shifting delightfully under the purple silk, and it took everything in Nathan's power not to drool. How could such a luscious woman even be real? It was as though she'd walked straight out of one of his video game worlds. "You know…yes. But no. If that makes sense?"

"You thought you were in love, but you found out later it wasn't?" Nathan guessed. He smiled his thanks as the waiter brought small plates out and placed them on the table. Aurora peered at the plates suspiciously.

"Nathan. There's no food on these plates," Aurora whispered, her eyes darting to the waiter's retreating back.

"He'll bring out the food and we can transfer it to these plates," Nathan said, tempering his smile.

"Oh good. I thought they were having a joke at our expense," Aurora said, relief visible on her face. "To answer your question – yes. I have loved before, but it was an innocent love, I suppose. Do you know those types of loves that are just…they aren't real? But they are beautiful for the moment because nothing can touch them?"

Nathan's stomach twisted at the way she spoke of another man. This was his own damn fault for bringing up this topic. But he listened dutifully and tried to understand what she was saying.

"You're saying a love that exists more in your head than in reality?" Nathan asked.

"Yes, that. Exactly. The idea of the love was perfect. We were young. It was fun. But we didn't really see each other, not truly. We enjoyed what we thought the other person was, but it was never real. Does that make sense?"

"Young love. Or first love," Nathan said. His angst eased a bit. He, too, had experienced a love like that. "When the person has no flaws and walks on clouds."

"That's not possible. You'd fall through a cloud," Aurora said, squinting at him.

"Erm, just a saying." Nathan laughed. He smiled as the waiter brought out a plate of bruschetta, warm bread with olive oil, and roasted artichokes. "I just mean that it seems like the person can do no wrong. That they are perfect in every way, but that's never really true. Nobody is perfect."

"You are," Aurora said, and Nathan's heart almost stopped. He caught her eyes, his mouth half open, and he wanted nothing more in the world than to kiss this stunning woman. Even more? He wanted to bundle her in cotton wool, take her home, and protect her from the world. He knew, with enough time, this innocence of hers would be lost as she explored new places. While he wanted to be the one to share in new discoveries with her, Nathan also feared that the more she learned of the world, the more she would realize just how many better options she had when it came to men. Insecurity reared its ugly head. Aurora was, quite literally, fresh off the boat from an extremely sheltered life on a remote island. Soon, she'd leave him behind when she discovered more. He'd just lucked out meeting her as quickly as he had.

"I don't think I'm perfect," Nathan said, shaking his head and keeping his tone light. "You're very sweet to say so. But we all have flaws. That's what makes us human."

A strange expression crossed her face, as though she smelled vinegar, and Nathan wondered why his words had bothered her so. He didn't want to upset her, and already he felt the date slipping away from him. Wanting to recapture the glow he'd felt, he reached across the table and took her hand.

"Aurora. I think you're the most incredible woman I've ever met. You light up this room, and I am the luckiest man in the world to be sitting across the table from you."

The smile returned to Aurora's face, and she squeezed his hand before leaning over to peer at the food.

"What should I start with?" Aurora asked, a crinkle in her brow.

"All of it," Nathan said. Picking up the dishes, he added a generous portion of each to her plate. "But, back to what we were talking about – I do know the feeling of first love. I've had it as well."

"You've loved before?" Aurora paused, an artichoke halfway to her mouth.

"I have. I'd say twice now. But, well, it wasn't returned." It stung to admit it, but in both cases of his more serious relationships, Nathan had come to realize over time that the women had not been as invested as he had been. That was the problem, Nathan realized. For all of his logic and awkwardness, as soon as he fell for a woman, he began building castles in the sky and dreaming of weddings. Sure, he was fantastical, but he liked to think he was hopeful. Because, at the end of the day, what was the point of life without hope?

"Isn't that sad?" Aurora said, her lower lip sticking out as though she was going to cry. Instantly empathetic, Aurora held still and waited for him to elaborate.

"I…well, yeah, I guess so. At the time, I was very sad. But you can't force someone to love you. And, I think, at the end of the day, it was for the best. I don't want to spend every day wondering if I'm good enough for my partner. Or if they're always looking out the door for someone else. I don't live well with uncertainty. I like things that make sense. Logic. Parameters. Rules." Nathan shook his head, laughing ruefully at himself.

"And these women didn't follow the rules of love. What are your rules?" Aurora asked. She finally ate the artichoke, and shock bloomed on her face.

"What's wrong?" Nathan leaned forward, worried.

"I…nothing. This is delicious." Aurora's eyes widened and she stabbed another artichoke with her fork, devouring it in seconds. "I can't believe how good this is."

"Oh, phew, I was worried something was wrong," Nathan said. Leaning back, he took a sip of his beer and scanned the restaurant as he thought about Aurora's question. Couples leaned into each other, laughing and talking, while a family in the corner argued heatedly over a topic. The night was warm, but the breeze was light, and soft music played in the background. "I guess my first rule of love is that I have to trust someone. Without trust, love can't really exist. Maybe there are types of love, like the unconditional love a parent has for their child – even if the child lies or struggles – but not in romantic love. At least not in my opinion. I think you can care for a partner that has broken your trust. But you'll never love them the same. If it's a big break, I guess. Like a foundational break in trust."

"So if someone hides a secret from you…you can't love them?" Aurora had stopped eating, her entire focus on his words.

"It depends on the secret, I guess," Nathan shrugged. "It's hard to say until I'm in the situation. But, yeah, I mean…if my girlfriend is with another man, then, that's not something I'm comfortable with moving past."

"Why would a woman have another partner if she is with you?" Aurora asked, indignant. Nathan, utterly charmed with her, let out a soft laugh.

"Sometimes people don't value what's right in front of them," Nathan said, his eyes on hers. "They're always looking for something more. Something better."

"I can understand that," Aurora said, that odd expression crossing her face again. "Maybe not with men, but with life. I wanted more. It's why I came here."

"Wanting to explore and grow in life is much different than actively deceiving your lover," Nathan said, understanding dawning.

"Oh, good." Aurora fell back against her chair, relieved, and looked at her empty plate. "I ate all the food. All of it. It's so good."

"There's more on the way. Don't worry – you can have

as much as you want," Nathan promised. "Speaking of... what do you want? For your future?"

Damn it all to hell and back, Nathan swore at himself. He was so caught up in this woman that it was like he was rushing to the finish line seconds after the starting bell.

"I want love," Aurora said automatically. She folded her hands in her lap and lifted those stunning turquoise eyes to his. "I want family. I want babies. But I also want freedom. I want to make my own choices without people telling me what to do. And I want to learn. I want to be with someone who helps me to learn, to explore, to see new things. I...I can't have a partner who will try to control me or force me into a way of life that I might not want. It's...I don't know how to say it."

"You want to be supported, but not controlled," Nathan surmised. There was a pause as the waiter brought out a large rough-hewn wood platter covered with food and small bowls.

"Our tasting menu has a variety of options," the waiter said. "We have smoked burrata, truffle pasta, roasted zucchini, coconut-curry risotto, grilled pineapple, spicy coleslaw, and an assortment of cheeses."

"I don't know what this all is," Aurora admitted, her eyes wide as the waiter went for another round of drinks.

"It's all vegetarian, so you should be able to enjoy it. Just try a little of each and see what you think."

"Thank you for sharing this with me, Nathan." Aurora leaned forward and licked her lips. Nathan almost fell out of his chair. Her words spun in his head, particularly about wanting a family and children. Nathan had always wanted to be a father – as he had a lot of love to give – but finding the right partner hadn't happened for him. Yet.

Now, looking across the table at Aurora, who seemingly shared the same hopes for the future and love, he made a promise to himself – that no matter what came, he was going to try and be the man she needed.

CHAPTER 9

"You look like you've eaten something distasteful," Aurora said. It was true, too, as Nathan held a pained look on his face. They stood on the side of the dance floor, shoulder to shoulder with other people who were also working up their courage to join the couples on the dance floor. Thirty minutes ago, a man with a large box in front of him had stepped on the stage. After fiddling with several switches and buttons, music had poured from what Nathan had referred to as the loudest speakers he'd ever heard before. While she was certain he exaggerated, Aurora did her best to hide her intrigue at the strange black boxes that now pumped out sultry salsa music. The beat of the music pulled her, pulsing gently in her core, but Nathan had held her back when she would have bounded onto the dance floor.

"Watch for a moment. It's a particular style of dance. One which I'm certain I'll butcher," Nathan muttered. He'd explained that salsa dancing had roots in various cultures but had originated on an island called Cuba. She watched as he pointed to where people moved their legs in sharp steps but kept their upper bodies largely still. Aurora could understand this dance – much like when she swam as a mermaid – her upper body remained still while her lower body was where her strength came from.

"And you've never tried this dance before?" Aurora looked up at Nathan, amusement slipping through her when his cheeks reddened.

"In all honesty? I've practiced at home. But never in public," Nathan admitted.

"You've practiced? How? With another woman?" A weird emotion worked its way through Aurora, something she wasn't familiar with. She realized that she didn't like the thought of Nathan with another woman. Which was unusual for her. Usually, everything in her life was so clear-cut. When it came to the past men in her life, either she was with them, or she wasn't. There was no uncertainty about the nature of their relationship. Being with Nathan, like this? There was uncertainty. She didn't know if he liked her – or if he would want a future with her. Aurora also didn't know much about his past, aside from what he'd told her, and it dawned on her now why trust was so important to humans.

The Mer, innately, did not lie or hide anything about their lives. Their tribe was small and worked together neatly as a unit for survival and the benefits of all. In doing so, it made it virtually impossible for a Mer to be dishonest, Aurora realized. It wasn't entirely unheard of, she supposed, as hadn't she snuck out against her parents' will? But she now understood a few things that she had taken for granted in how a society operated. Here, with so many people coming from so many backgrounds, Aurora could understand why Mirra had advised her to proceed with caution. How was she to know if someone spoke truths or lies to her? While she trusted her gut instincts, as the Mer were highly attuned beings, Aurora would need to careful.

"No, not with another woman," Nathan said. He laughed and ran a hand through his hair, causing the dark strands to stand up in little tufts. He looked like a disgruntled bird, his glasses half-tilted on his nose, and Aurora wanted to cuddle in close to him. Maybe not everyone in this world was to be trusted, but she felt Nathan could be. Everything in her told her that the man before her was a genuinely good person. Which to her was the most attractive thing in the world. "Um, in front of the mirror. I just put the music on and tried some steps. I figured, since I live here now and this is very popular, that maybe I should, you know, well…"

"Nathan! Were you trying to teach yourself to dance in case you were to meet a woman?" Aurora exclaimed, threading her arm through his. She liked how warm and solid he felt against her. Nathan towered over her, his broad shoulders and wide body shielding her from the crowd behind them, and the desire to snuggle into him rose once more.

"I was," Nathan said. "I'm not sure what the point of that was, because I missed a very important step."

"What's that?"

"Well, two steps, actually…" Nathan grinned down at her, and her lips curved in response. "First, work up courage to leave my house and actually go dancing. Second, find a willing woman to dance with me."

"Looks like you have both tonight," Aurora declared. She squeezed his bicep and tugged him onto the dance floor, separating him from the line of people who clapped on the side of the dance floor. "Your time has arrived. This is the moment you've been waiting for."

"You know what?" Nathan surprised her by snaking an arm around her waist and grabbing one of her hands, pulling her close. Heat speared her where their bodies pressed together, and Aurora went dizzy for a moment, blinking up at him. She'd never felt this way with someone before, unsettled and yet, absolutely certain. Was this what love felt like? It was like she wanted to pull Nathan close and never let go, and at the same time, run and hide.

This man could change her world.

It was terrifying, really, to realize the power another person could have over the trajectory of her life, Aurora thought. Nerves tumbled in her stomach.

"I think that you're right. This *is* the moment I've been waiting for," Nathan said, drawing her attention back to him. His words struck her, and Aurora threw caution to the wind. Maybe she'd need to be slow to trust other people, but not this man. Both a curious mix of shy and eager, Nathan gulped air like a fish out of water, and Aurora suppressed a giggle. They waited while the man chattered to the crowd, yelling something unintelligible that got the crowd excited and cheering, and then launched into another song.

"One, two, three…. four," Nathan muttered under his breath as he guided her backward in time to the music.

"Are you counting the steps?" Aurora exclaimed. She'd studied the women on the dance floor while they had waited, and now she fell automatically into the dance.

"It helps me to remember," Nathan admitted. He moved his hips against hers in a sexy little swivel, and Aurora gasped in delight. Dancing was fun, she realized, and kept up with the beat. When Nathan stumbled, a dark cloud crossed his face.

"Don't think," Aurora said. Reaching up, she held a palm to his cheek, drawing his gaze down to her lips. She stopped the dance, needing him to connect with her, and stretched up on her toes to steal a kiss. For a moment, they stood there, dancers swirling around them as the music pulsed a sultry beat, the kiss drawing out. *Him*, her heart seemed to whisper. When a man whistled sharply by them, Aurora drew back, breaking the kiss. "You feel that?"

Nathan only nodded.

"Take that...and dance." Aurora drew backwards, bringing Nathan with her until he caught the beat, and then allowed him to lead her into the dance. She knew the moment that he finally let go, stopped counting steps, and let himself just feel. The shift was subtle, but all of a sudden they were working as a team, their bodies brushing lightly as they followed the music. Aurora found that she loved dancing on land – perhaps even more so than in water – because it allowed her to be close to Nathan. Feeling his strong body lead her through the dance only heightened her pleasure, shooting a sexy little thrill through her.

As the song ended, the crowd gave a collective cheer, encouraging the man to play another and he happily complied. Now, the music slowed, and more people joined the dance floor, forcing her and Nathan closer together. Aurora didn't mind, she'd take any moment she could in his arms, and pressed herself against his chest. He smelled like soap and something deeper, a spicy scent that had Aurora nuzzling closer. Heat bloomed between them, as they swayed, hip-to-hip, no longer trying to keep on the beat of the music.

The night took on a magickal quality for Aurora, which was saying something since magick was second nature to her. Maybe it was the newness of it all, or maybe it was Nathan, but Aurora experienced a curious mix of giddiness and anticipation. The balmy air drifted around them, carrying the scent of decadent foods, and the lanterns hung alongside the bar shimmered in the night. The music drifted behind them, forgotten, as Nathan moved her gently to the corner of the dance floor, so they didn't bump into other people. There, in the shadows, he kissed her.

This kiss...it felt different than the others. Nathan took charge, angling her head so that the kiss deepened – just for a moment – and Aurora lost herself to the sensations that flooded her body. She wanted him, of that much she was certain, but it was more than that. Her skin hummed where he stroked his hands lightly down her back, and she wanted to feel his touch everywhere on her body. Nathan kissed with a single-minded intensity that told her, instinctively, that he would be a good lover. But did she want him for more than that? Was it even a possibility for them to have a relationship?

Aurora made a soft sound of distress at the thought,

and Nathan immediately broke the kiss, looking around at the other people on the dance floor.

"I'm sorry – it's probably not the best place for me to kiss you," Nathan said, misinterpreting her.

"I like kissing you," Aurora said, raising her eyes to his. She traced a finger over his cheek and down his chest. "I'd like to do more of it. Dancing is good for you, Nathan. Once you relaxed, you did a great job. Will you dance with me some more?" Aurora worried that Nathan would end the night early, and she felt revved-up, like she could dance until the morning, and didn't want the night to end. When she was dancing, she didn't have to answer any questions or pretend that she knew all the things that he was talking about.

"Of course." Nathan drew his chin up and adopted a haughty look as the DJ moved into a faster song. "Let's see if you can keep up with me."

"Is that a challenge?" Aurora liked seeing this side of him, where he stopped getting in his head and just lived in the moment.

"It is. I have it on good authority that women like men who can dance. Finally, it's my moment to shine." Nathan's lips quirked, letting Aurora know he was teasing, but she wasn't going to let him back down now.

"Okay then, bring it on, tough guy. Let's see what you've got," Aurora threw up her hands and shimmied into the middle of the crowd.

CHAPTER 10

"*I* don't know…I think I held my own," Nathan protested. They were walking the boulevard that ran along the water, having stayed until the bar closed, and now they wandered toward Nathan's villa. True to his word, he didn't want to drive after the drinks he had enjoyed, and Aurora had surprised him by suggesting she accompany him home. He wanted her to come with him – in fact he was certain he wanted her around at all times – but hadn't wanted to seem presumptuous about asking. Now, knowing she was feeling the same way toward him, well, at the very least not interested in ending the night yet, a hum of pleasure rippled through him.

He'd seen the looks at the bar. Every man in the room had eyes on Aurora. And, more than once, he'd seen the questioning look in their eyes when they spotted who she was dancing with. He didn't blame them, not really, for Aurora was just *that* incredible. There was no man that could do her justice, so at the very least he didn't have to feel that insecure when people gave him those looks. He agreed with them. And wasn't he about the luckiest man in the world to have her on his arm? It had made his chest swell with pride, and he'd found that he'd felt more confident as the night went on. Maybe that was just the power of a beautiful and sweet woman who had eyes only for him. It wasn't a feeling he'd had before, and he wanted to capture this night and bottle it up, never forgetting just how Aurora had made him feel.

Like he was the only man for her.

He'd watched her, too. Helpless not to question if she looked at other men or invited other flirtations while he'd gone to the bar for drinks. But, while she'd looked around with that ever-curious gaze of hers, she'd spoken to no one else and hadn't even glanced in another man's direction. When he'd come back from the bar, drinks in hand, her face would light with pleasure – making him feel like a million dollars.

Was there a better feeling than someone you loved smiling when you crossed a room to them? Nathan caught his toe on a crack in the sidewalk at the thought of love, and Aurora steadied him with a chuckle.

"Careful. You don't want to get hurt," Aurora said.

"I can be a klutz sometimes," Nathan said. He squeezed her hand, enjoying how she automatically squeezed it back. A sound from the ocean caught his attention. Aurora skidded to a stop, turning toward the water.

Inky black, except for where a few streetlights shone into the shallows, the surface of the ocean rocked gently, holding her own secrets. Nathan always wondered what mysteries lay dormant in those depths, and he promised himself – for the thousandth time – that one day he would learn to swim so he could explore more deeply. The sound rose again, a haunting call that sent a shiver down his spine, and he tilted his head at Aurora's small gasp.

"What is that? It sounds like a bird…or maybe it's a boat horn?" Nathan asked. He studied Aurora. Gone was the lighthearted woman he'd just danced with for hours, and instead, a furrow marred her pretty face as she worried her lower lip.

"It's…" Aurora shook her head and stopped.

"You know it?" Nathan asked.

"It's a mother calling for her baby," Aurora bit out and turned away from the water, her arms crossed over her chest. Nathan followed her as she stomped along the sidewalk, not sure what had changed exactly, but the mood was different now.

"A mother what?" Nathan asked. When he received no response, he tried to wade through the undercurrent of emotions that he was receiving from Aurora. Maybe the sound made her think of home? "Do you miss your mother? You didn't speak of your parents much. Are you close?"

"Not in the way I'd like to be," Aurora shrugged one shoulder, the movement sharp, and Nathan threaded his arm through hers, wanting to be close to her. He sensed she needed comfort but wasn't sure what she would allow.

"I'm sorry. Family can be difficult, can't it?"

"She expects too much of me. She always tells – but never asks. What I want, what my needs are? They aren't important to her. Or if they are…she's never made it known. Fall in line, do what is expected of you. That is the best course of action, always." Aurora's words were clipped, and they'd picked up speed a bit as she dragged him further away from the water and the haunting call that drifted on the night's breeze.

"I'm guessing she wasn't pleased about your trip to Siren Island then?" Nathan wasn't sure if he should press the topic or not, but one thing he did know about women? A silent one was more dangerous than one that was speaking. If he could keep Aurora talking, maybe she wouldn't get too upset.

"That's likely an understatement," Aurora muttered. Nathan drew her away from the beach, and down the road that led to his villa. Once the water was no longer in sight, shut out by the crowded homes and lush gardens that hugged this street, Aurora visibly relaxed.

"I, for one, am delighted you made the trip," Nathan said, bumping her shoulder lightly with his. When a small smile appeared on her face, he breathed out a sigh of relief. Now, if he could just distract her long enough – hopefully he could keep her from falling into a sad mood. She'd had her fair share of drinks this evening, too, and he knew how alcohol could exacerbate a sour mood. "It's this one."

"This is your place?" Aurora stopped in front of a small white villa with large windows, wooden shutters, and palm trees lining the garden. An old-fashioned bell with a hanging rope served as the doorbell, and a ship's wheel was the door handle on the arched front door.

"Yes, I don't own it. I just rent it. I've just extended my lease so that I can stay another year."

"You like Siren Island then?" Aurora asked as he fished the key from his pocket and unlocked the door.

"I do. I mean, there are some things that are inconvenient about living here, but I find I've been really productive. It's good for my work. And good for my brain. We'll see what another year brings." *And I hope you're in it,* Nathan added silently.

"This place is nice!" Aurora exclaimed, wandering through the small foyer to the open concept living area. Set up so that the large floor-to-ceiling windows on two sides of the house could catch the wind, as well as give a beautiful view to the ocean, the main room had a wraparound couch, a weathered wood dining table, and a beautiful kitchen with a breakfast bar. The floors were a dark grey washed concrete, with a few colorful rugs tossed around. A staircase at the foyer led upstairs to the two bedrooms – one of which he used for his office. Nathan spent most of his time in his office, but he loved coming downstairs, particularly late at night and walking out onto the expansive deck. There, he would dangle his legs into the small lap pool while he leaned back and looked up at the stars.

Since the sound they'd heard on the ocean distressed Aurora so, Nathan decided against showing her the outside. What he really wanted to do was take her to his bedroom, but didn't want to be crass in asking her to do so. He found himself caught in his awkwardness, uncertain how to proceed with this incredible goddess who had landed in his life.

Turning from where she scanned the room, Aurora tilted her head in consideration.

"Where do you sleep?" Aurora asked.

"Um, there's a bedroom upstairs. And my office."

"Will you show me?" Aurora walked across the room,

stopping inches away from him, causing his thoughts to scramble.

"Um…"

"No? Is it too private?"

"Of course not." Though Nathan did a quick run-through to try and remember if he'd left anything embarrassing out in his bedroom. But laundry day had been two days ago, and the cleaner had come through recently, so there shouldn't be anything amiss. Grabbing her hand, he pulled her up the stairs and dragged her past his messy office and into his bedroom.

It was a nice space, with the large bed set against a long accent wall painted a dark blue. The bed faced large balcony doors that opened to the sea, and simple gauzy white curtains framed them. He'd even made the bed today, a feat for which he patted himself on the back, considering his lack of sleep the night before. Honestly, Nathan was surprised he wasn't falling over at this point – he was beyond tired – but being with Aurora seemed to light him up in a way that coffee had never quite achieved. He was buzzing with anticipation and nerves, and not entirely sure how he should proceed. If he wanted Aurora in his life, it would be best that he not have any expectations…

Nathan let out a whoosh of air as Aurora jumped him. He stumbled backwards, his arms coming around her waist, as she hitched her legs up on his waist and settled her arms around his neck. Grateful that he was a strong man, for a woman like Aurora deserved a man who could hold her, he cradled her close. Aurora's lips were on his, giving him no time to think, and he walked backward until the back of his knees hit the edge of the bed. Torn between the intensity of her kisses, and not wanting to drop her, he tore his mouth away.

"Hold on," Nathan advised, and Aurora grinned at him, tightening her arms around his neck as he toppled back onto the bed, bouncing lightly against the firm mattress.

Nathan was certain he'd died and gone to heaven.

The reality of Aurora, across the dinner table or dancing with him, was one thing. But having all her gloriousness spread out over him? It was like the one time he'd gone to Comic Con and the over stimulation of seeing all of his favorite characters in one place had caused him to freeze until his assistant had rescued him from his stupor. At least this time, instinct took over for him.

When Aurora leaned down for a kiss, her hair falling in silky threads around her head and curtaining his face, Nathan slowed her movements. Instead of devouring, he sampled, her lips a dessert to be savored. A soft mewling escaped her, and she gasped against his mouth, shifting her hips so that she connected with where he'd already grown hard in anticipation. The movement shot a million electrical bolts to his brain, and it took all his power to slow the pace and not be overcome with desire.

He wanted to take his time with Aurora. It was important to him that he learn her reactions, what she liked, and what he could do to excite her. Because of that, he caught her hands when she started to tug at his shirt, whimpering against his mouth, as she rotated those lush hips over him. It killed him, it really did, but he rolled her off him so that she was on her back on the bed.

"Nathan?" Aurora asked. She pushed that sexy lower

lip of hers out in a pout. Helpless not to, Nathan angled himself over her and nipped at that same lip, sucking gently. She hummed lightly against his mouth, a sound of pleasure, and he moved back. Their eyes met. What he saw there, nothing but desire and excitement for him – *him* – awkward computer nerd Nathan, made him feel incredible.

"I want to slow this down," Nathan said. He trailed his lips across her jaw, and across the nape of her neck, sucking lightly against her sweetly scented skin. A soft sigh escaped her mouth, and Nathan noted this as a sensitive spot to pay attention to. He lingered there, inhaling her delicious scent and pressing soft kisses to her neck, while running a hand lightly up and down her side. She had such an exciting body to touch, the silk sliding over her soft waist and generous thighs. Hers was a body made for touching, and Nathan delighted in the experience as she squirmed under his hands. Sitting back, Nathan moved so that he straddled her, and then lifted one of her arms as she watched him with lustful eyes. "Have I told you how beautiful you are?"

"Yes, you have." A smile dimpled Aurora's stunning face.

"It's more than just physical though," Nathan said. Removing his glasses, he tossed them further up the bed. He pressed a kiss to the inside of her wrist, lingering when she squirmed under him, and then traced his lips up the sensitive inside of her arm. "It's your spirit, Aurora. You meet the world as a challenge...as an opportunity. You have an infectious enthusiasm, and yet carry a kind heart."

"Oh, Nathan," Aurora said on a sigh.

"It's easy to compliment you on your physical beauty."

Nathan's lips found her collarbone once more, and then he dipped lower, capturing her hardened nipple through the silk dress with his mouth. Wetting the fabric, he sucked lightly, as Aurora arched against him. "But it's clear to see that your soul matches if not exceeds that beauty." Nathan berated himself for a second, wishing he had a better way with words, and instead pressed a kiss between her breasts where her heart was.

"Nathan…you're so sweet to me. I feel safe with you…in a way that I don't think I could with others. I think…I think…" Aurora trailed off as Nathan captured her other nipple, both of his hands cupping her heavy breasts. Testing their weight, he stroked them, relishing in their fullness. When Aurora didn't continue, Nathan chuckled at her breast.

"Yes, Aurora?"

"I…oh, goddess, but that feels soooo good…" Aurora moaned, writhing beneath him as he steadfastly focused on worshiping her breasts. "I think…I think…"

"Yes, Aurora?" Nathan wondered if she would be a woman who could climax from stimulating her breasts alone, but when she whimpered in frustration, he decided to continue his exploration instead. Placing his hands on the bed, he eased himself off of her until he was kneeling between where her legs dangled at the edge of the bed. Nathan hooked his hands behind her thighs and pulled her close to him.

"No, Nathan…" Aurora levered herself up on her elbows, her hair a tumbled mess around her shoulders. Her face was set in a lovely mix of frustration and desire, and already her lips looked swollen from his kisses. She looked rumpled and grumpy, and Nathan found he enjoyed keeping her slightly off-kilter. In the little time since she blew into his world, Aurora had dominated, and he'd delightfully followed along in enthusiastic explorations. But here? Now he would be the one to lead.

Placing a hand on her stomach, he pushed her lightly back onto the bed and inched her skirt up her legs. Caressing the soft skin of her inner thighs, he licked her skin lightly and then blew on it, delighting when her legs jerked. Oh, yes. She was very responsive, which helped lead him where he wanted to go most. Easing the rest of the silk upwards, Nathan lifted a brow at her lack of underwear. It was a good thing he hadn't known she was completely nude under this dress, though he'd already made a fair guess at the lack of bra. Now though? Even though he wanted to linger, Nathan brought his mouth to her, tasting her sweetness, and was rewarded when Aurora's hips bucked. Slowly, he sampled her, licking and stroking, over and over until she cried out, rearing up off the bed before collapsing back. Her thighs trembled around his ears, and still Nathan feasted, wanting to bring her once more to the precipice. One was never enough, he thought, pulling his mouth back and lightly blowing on her sensitive skin.

"Nathan…" Aurora panted.

"I love how you taste," Nathan decided, looking up at her. She'd shifted to her elbows again, and her turquoise eyes were heavy with desire. He held her eyes and slid a finger inside of her, and Aurora moaned and fell back to the bed. Bending over, Nathan continued to feast.

Since he tended to like numbers in groupings of threes,

Nathan stayed where he was until he brought Aurora pleasure not once, but twice. Satisfied that she'd enjoyed herself, Nathan eased back with a smile on his face. Standing, he walked to the side of the bed and pulled the sheet back, motioning for her to cross to him.

"That was…" Aurora shook her head. "I have no words. Incredible. Mind-blowing? Amazing?"

"I'll take it. Here…come here." Nathan crawled beneath the sheet and patted his shoulder. Aurora took the invite and dove beneath the covers to snuggle into him.

"Now I think it is your turn?" Aurora looked up at him, a gleam in her eye.

"No, Aurora. Tonight was about you. I want you to know that I will always want to put your pleasure first."

"But…" Aurora tilted her head, surprise etched on her face.

"I'm just fine, Aurora. This isn't the first time I've gone to sleep like this."

"But you are still unsatisfied…" Aurora protested.

"Oh, trust me…I'm more than satisfied. Pleasing you pleases me."

"Really?" Aurora squinted at him.

"Really. Plus, I am exhausted. We have time to build up to these things. Let's linger over this dance a bit longer…right?"

"Oh, that does sound nice. But, I really want to have sex with you, Nathan. I know it will feel so good for the both of us." Aurora with her directness, nearly undid him, but Nathan only shook his head and pulled her close.

"And we can look forward to how good it will feel then. Anticipation is a good thing."

"Is it? But I want it now," Aurora argued, and Nathan laughed.

"You are good for my ego, Aurora. I really like you and I enjoyed tonight. Do you want to sleep here, next to me?"

"I do," Aurora said, a grumpy note still lingering in her voice. "Maybe tomorrow I'll convince you to have sex with me."

"When we have sex Aurora?" Nathan waited until her eyes met his. "It's going to be *more* than just sex. Understood?"

He was asleep before he even heard her answer.

CHAPTER 11

"*I* think I love him," Aurora said as she rushed into the kitchen the next morning after Nathan had dropped her at The Laughing Mermaid. Rumpled, confused, and nervous, Aurora had barged into the kitchen in a whirlwind of angst. Jolie simply smirked and crossed the kitchen to pour an extra cup of coffee, while Mirra immediately wrapped her arms around Aurora.

"You don't seem too pleased about this," Mirra said. She held Aurora a moment longer, swaying gently with her, before pulling back to study Aurora's face. "You are, however, glowing."

"Good sex will do that to a woman," Jolie commented as she placed the coffee cup on the table and pointed to a chair. "Sit. I'll make you breakfast."

Two different ways to nurture, Aurora realized, and both very much appreciated in their own way. Following instructions, Aurora sat and sipped the fragrant coffee, and tried to gather her thoughts.

"Why don't you tell us what happened?" Mirra asked. She looked cool and fresh in a mint green top tucked into loose linen pants, her white-blond hair braided back from her face.

"We had dinner. We talked for hours. We danced for hours longer. We...well..."

"Knocked boots?" Jolie suggested, plopping butter in a pan on the stove.

"I'm not wearing boots?" Aurora looked at Jolie in question.

"It's just a weird saying for having sex...getting laid is another common one you'll hear," Mirra said. She squeezed Aurora's hand. "Go on."

"Well, we didn't do that. Not all of it at least. He only wanted to pleasure me. He wouldn't let me give him pleasure and he said no to sex. Then he fell asleep immediately."

"I knew I liked him," Jolie declared as she popped some bread in a toaster.

"This is a good thing?" Aurora asked. She didn't see how it could be. She'd stayed up much of the rest of the night worrying she'd done something to upset him.

"Well, yes, in Nathan's case? Likely so," Mirra said. "I'm guessing he is trying to take it slow...well, slow-ish, to show you that he respects you. Here, sometimes if men move too fast, it can indicate to a woman that they only want sex. So, maybe he pumped the brakes a bit just to show he cares."

"Pumped the brakes, I keep hearing that phrase. That is for the car, right? The slowing down mechanism?" Aurora asked.

"Correct." Jolie's lips quirked, but she didn't say anything else.

"Yes, well, he did mention that building anticipation was important. And that when we did have sex it would mean more than just sex."

"Ah, there it is," Mirra patted her hand cheerfully. "He wants to make love to you, Aurora. Which means he wants to give you some time to build something together."

"I…I think I already love him though. How does it work here? How do I know? I've never felt this way before." Aurora rubbed a hand to her stomach where a bundle of nerves had formed, twisting in knots like two eels fighting for a fish.

"Tell me how you feel," Jolie instructed. She added peppers and onions to the frying pan and soon a fragrant scent filled the kitchen.

"Sick to my stomach? Scared? Giddy? Happy?"

"Yes, that does sound right," Jolie said.

"But…is it too soon? How would this even work? I can't…I can't just…" Panic slithered from the knot in her stomach and gripped at her chest, and Aurora took several deep breaths to calm herself while Mirra rubbed her back.

"Shhh, honey, it's okay. Listen to me…" Mirra turned Aurora to face her. "There is no timeframe on love. Only you get to decide that. It can happen like a lightning bolt or take years to build. You need to focus on how you feel, and then think about what you want. After that, you'll need to have a conversation with Nathan about what *he* wants and if he feels the same."

"He was talking about trust…about how it's so important to him. And for a good relationship," Aurora said, twisting the bracelet he'd given her. "I'm not being truthful with him."

"But..." Mirra paused as Jolie brought plates piled with eggs and toast over to the table.

"Here's the thing, Aurora. Nathan's not wrong about wanting to establish trust in a relationship. But you're also not wrong for concealing who you are from him. You must do that in order to protect yourself. It's actually a very real safety concern. If Nathan feels the same way back, he'll understand why you didn't share that with him. I mean, you've known the guy...what? All of two minutes? You can't exactly throw the mermaid stuff at him right away."

"Forty hours..." Aurora squinted at the clock on the wall. "In human time that is."

"See? That's another thing – he'll have a huge adjustment to learn and accept about the Mer. Like how time moves differently there. It's not just another time zone – it's another world." Jolie plopped down in the chair across from Aurora and took a piece of toast from the plate.

"And you think he won't accept it?" Aurora asked. *Or accept me?* The last thought brought sadness to her heart. She wasn't used to being in a position where someone might judge her and find her wanting. The Mer generally thrived on lifting each other up and working together as a community.

"We don't know." Mirra shrugged and took a sip of her coffee. "Tell me...why him? What do you like about him?"

"Oh, well, he's thoughtful. He listens to me, like really listens to me. Then he'll ask me questions and listen some more. I've never had that...not where someone doesn't know who I am and feels they have to listen to me because I'm the princess. It's like…without the label of that sitting on my shoulders, I'm able to just be me. And he sees me. He laughs at my poor attempts at jokes. He's patient with the fact that I don't understand a lot of this world…" Aurora trailed off when Jolie lifted a finger.

"How did you explain that?"

"He knows the Triste Islands are very small and largely uninhabited. So, he thinks I'm just very sheltered," Aurora said. She nibbled on a piece of toast, hoping to soothe the nerves in her stomach.

"That's not a bad explanation." Jolie pursed her lips and thought it over. "And, if you're saying that he's patient and helpful, well, those are both really good things."

"He's smart, too. I don't understand his work at all, but he promised to show me. He remembers the things that I say and then brings them up later. And he's shy. I like that about him. He makes me want to bring him out of his shell, have fun…live a little."

"Yeah, it's love," Jolie said to Mirra who beamed.

"Congrats, Aurora, this all sounds wonderful," Mirra said.

"Does it? Because…I can't…how do I?" Aurora threw up her hands. "It doesn't make sense. It can't make sense. He can't even swim. How in the world will we be together? I can't just run away from home forever."

"Can't you?" Jolie asked and then winced when Mirra smacked her arm.

"Don't encourage her," Mirra hissed.

"Well, she needs to know her options, doesn't she?" Jolie insisted. She tucked a dark lock of hair behind her ear and leaned forward, elbows on the table, and grasped both of Aurora's hands. "Listen to me, Aurora."

"Yes." Aurora met Jolie's eyes and even though she had been tough with her to start, Aurora trusted Jolie.

"You need to understand that you have choices. It may seem like you don't, but I'm telling you that you do. If you do not want to go home and want to figure out a way to live on Siren Island – I…"

"We…" Mirra interjected.

"*We*," Jolie continued, "will help you. But you need to think about what that will mean. Will your family be upset? Can someone else step into a leadership role? What happens to your people? If you want to make this decision, you can certainly do so – but you also need to be an adult about it. Which means you need to talk to your parents and tell them what your choice will be. They can't keep you as a prisoner. It may be a difficult choice to make, but you have to hear me when I say that you do have options. That's where you start. Because you can't go to Nathan, tell him you love him, and then walk away without an explanation. That…would be…"

"Cruel," Aurora said. Jolie nodded.

"I always thought I'd have to stay in our village and be the princess. I didn't know I could have more. Nobody ever told me," Aurora said. A mixture of excitement and confusion made her stomach turn, and she grabbed for her piece of toast again. Chewing the crusty bread for a moment, she thought it over. They were right. While she'd only just arrived at Siren Island, she'd lucked out in finding fellow Mer to take her in and guide her. But what would have happened if they hadn't?

Would she feel differently about staying on land if she hadn't been able to see that other Mer were successfully living this way? Now that she knew the new life that awaited her, it seemed almost impossible to think about going home. It helped to hear Jolie tell her that she had choices.

"I think...times are changing. The Mer are going to explore more and more," Mirra said. "My mother is marrying Ezra, and right now I think they're in Portugal. Can you imagine it? We used to think we couldn't travel much, and now we know we can connect with Mer all over the world. Granted, there's safety restrictions with our travel and we need to stay close to water...just in case. But still! It's a fabulous time for our people."

"And potentially a scary one. If the Mer aren't smart about how to adjust to living..." Jolie's eyes widened. She snapped her fingers. "Wait just a minute..."

"What?" Mirra tilted her head as her sister pulled out her phone and tapped it. Aurora still hadn't worked up the courage to ask anyone to play on this device yet, but she had *so* many questions about how it worked. When a voice sounded from the little box, Aurora's eyes widened.

"Hi girls!" The voice said and Jolie stood and walked to sit between Aurora and Mirra and held the device in front of them. There, a tiny woman and man waved at them. Aurora dipped her head, looking behind the device, and then back at the front. What magick was this? Were they trapped in the phone?

"Mom, this is Aurora. She's Mer from Triste Islands. We rescued her from the beach before she made any catastrophic mistakes," Jolie said.

Aurora turned and glared at Jolie who just bumped her shoulder against hers.

"Hi Aurora. I'm Irma and this is Ezra." Irma, a stunning woman with silvery hair and luminous eyes smiled at Aurora. The man next to her squinted his eyes in thought. When he spoke, his voice sounded different, as though he sounded his words out a different way.

"Triste Islands...if I remember correctly...you wouldn't happen to be the princess, would you?" Ezra asked, holding his hand to his chin.

"I am," Aurora squeaked.

"What's wrong?" Mirra whispered.

"How do they fit in that box?" Aurora asked. She didn't care if it sounded stupid, she really needed to know.

"Oh, of course," Mirra began.

"See? This is what I'm calling about," Jolie said. "Aurora doesn't understand how a phone with video works. She doesn't know about the internet. Or the fact that you aren't actually in the phone but using a device to communicate from Portugal."

"There is a steep learning curve when you first come to land," Irma agreed. "But that's okay, honey. We all learn at our own pace."

"That's what I'm thinking though!" Jolie said, excitement evident on her face. "Ted, my delightful love, who is like, the smartest guy in the world, also knows how to teach. I just had this idea for creating an actual program – where we teach Mer how to acclimate to the land if they choose to do so."

Aurora's mouth dropped open. Silence filled the kitchen, as apparently Jolie had stunned everyone else as well. The idea had merit, Aurora thought, knowing just how uncomfortable she felt navigating what seemed to be simple situations for most people. She thought back to yesterday and what a crowning achievement buying ice cream was. Such a simple thing, too, and yet it had brought a round of nerves with it.

"I don't know, Jolie," Irma said, shaking her head. "Wouldn't that just be opening the floodgates for the Mer to leave the ocean? I can see there being a lot of push-back with something like this."

"But..." Mirra said, raising a finger. "The Mer are going to do it anyway. Look at Aurora. She found her way here. The Mer *are* already doing it. This isn't a bad idea. At the very least, we could make it safer for a Mer to try this out. Not everyone is going to like living in this world. But curiosity happens. And maybe this would be a way to make it safe?"

"That's what I'm saying..." Jolie smiled with approval for Mirra's words. "They are already doing it. We can provide a roadmap. Your company can do this, can't it Ezra? Hire us. I'm putting all three of our names in for jobs."

"Wait...what?" Aurora shot a startled look at Jolie.

"You'd be our test case. We can figure it all out with you and you can earn money while doing so. You'll need it to live here if you plan to stay."

"My own money?" Aurora had not once considered the fact that she could earn money, let alone the fact that she would need it to survive on Siren Island. What a silly thing to not consider, she realized, as she'd seen people exchanging money everywhere they went. Of course she would need to earn money to live.

"I like it. We'll need to iron out the pitfalls and discuss how to frame it up. Why don't you put a proposal together for me and we'll discuss salaries after I review it?" Ezra asked, making his decision quickly.

"Delighted to be working with you, Ezra. Love you, Mom! Don't worry, we have everything handled here!" Jolie blew kisses at the phone and then ended the call.

"What just happened?" Mirra wondered.

"I…"—Jolie pointed to her chest— "am a problem solver. I figured out a way for Aurora to make money, and she doesn't have to depend on Nathan. That makes her life a little easier because she can decide to stay here now whether things work out with him or not. I also figured out a way to be of help to our people so that more Mer aren't putting themselves in harm's way. This is good. I was looking for a new project."

"I'm not sure that I was…" Mirra said faintly.

"Oh come on, this will be great. Ladies…we've got work to do. Aurora?" Jolie lifted an eyebrow in question.

"I'd hug you, but you're kind of scary. I'll just say thank you instead."

At the sound of barking outside, Jolie rose.

"That's Ted back with Snowy. I'm going to steal him away for a few hours to talk about this and then we can set up a work schedule. Oh…Aurora, what are your plans tonight?"

"I don't know…" Aurora jumped as a furry bolt of energy zipped into the room and tumbled at Jolie's feet.

"That's my sweet baby," Jolie said, bending to pet the

adoring dog. Aurora fell instantly in love and decided that if she moved here, she was getting one of these animals as well. "We can meet tonight if you'd like?"

"I…I think I may need to go in the water tonight." Aurora clamped her lips shut when a man walked through the door. He was handsome in a buttoned-up kind of way, but his entire face lit with pleasure when he saw Jolie.

"Ted, this is Aurora. She's Mer and facing some difficult choices. We are going to help her," Jolie said as she wound an arm around his waist.

"I'm happy to help in any way that I can," Ted said to her, his eyes serious.

"We can just…" Aurora looked to Mirra and then back to Ted.

"Yes, he's well aware of everything mermaid. It's one of his favorite subject matters, actually. He writes books and stuff. Smarty-pants." Jolie beamed up at him and kissed his cheek, causing Ted's cheeks to pinken.

"It can work. Between humans and Mer? It really can." Aurora said it more as a statement than a question and blew out a breath. "That's good news…isn't it?"

"I'll fill you in," Jolie whispered to Ted when he opened his mouth.

"I need to go in the water tonight, I think. I heard my parents last night. Over the ocean. They were calling for me." Aurora still felt horrible about walking away from their call.

"I'll go with you," Mirra said immediately.

"And I," Jolie agreed.

"But…"

"You don't have to do this alone. And we'll come to

show them that you're in safe hands right now. You need to go, though. It's not fair to them to not at least tell them where you are," Mirra said.

"I know, I know. I felt...feel...horrible." Aurora wrung her hands.

"It'll be okay. We'll figure this out. We'll go tonight and find them. Why don't you go to your room and rest for a bit? Take some time just for you and collect your thoughts. We'll tackle one problem at a time...together."

CHAPTER 12

*A*urora spent the afternoon devouring magazines that the guests had left behind. She pulled the entire stack from the communal bookshelves in the hall-way, wanting to also use the pictures as a way to absorb what life on land was like. She was so engrossed in flipping through the glossy pages, that she barely heard the knock at her door.

"Hey," Mirra poked her head in when Aurora responded.

"Hi," Aurora said. "I'm just doing a quick study of these to see what I can learn."

"I see," Mirra said. She raised an eyebrow at one of the gossip magazines Aurora held up. "Well, it's certainly a part of society – but not all of it. These are the famous people."

"Famous for what? Being Queens?" Aurora studied a woman who wore a glittery dress that barely covered her butt.

"They wish…" Mirra laughed. "A lot of them are actors and actresses."

"I'm not familiar…" Aurora shook her head.

"Of course, so you probably haven't watched a movie or a television show?" Mirra shook her head and glanced at the window where the last of the sun's rays kissed the sky. "Listen, that's a whole different type of entertainment that we'll show you when we have time. Basically, it's like storytelling through physically acting it out. And then you use costumes and sets…it creates a whole mood. It's recorded, so people can watch it at different times on their devices."

"Like on the phone?" Aurora asked. Now she wanted to see a movie.

"Correct. I promise we'll do a movie night soon, but we should get in the water. If your parents moved on to the next islands, we might have a good swim ahead of us tonight."

"You're certain you want to come? I can go on my own. I'm used to dealing with them," Aurora said. She really wanted Jolie and Mirra to join her, but in her old life people were always doing what she wanted because she was a princess. Here she wanted people to do things with her because they chose to do so. Because, at the end of the day, if she stayed – she'd no longer be royalty. Which meant she'd have to learn to do things on her own. The idea was more exciting than unnerving, and that told Aurora a lot about where her heart lay. Not just with Nathan, but also for what she wanted for her future.

"Of course we are going to come with you. I suspect it will help reassure your parents that you're safe to be here with us and maybe they won't try to force you to come home with them," Mirra said.

"That's what I'm hoping," Aurora said. The sound of the waves hitting the sand carried to her on the breeze, and the ocean called to her – as it always did.

"Nathan called for you. We realized that without a phone, you don't really have a way to communicate with him. We'll have to remedy that once you speak to your parents, but for now he's wondering if you'd like to have dinner tomorrow? He'll pick you up if so."

"If I can stay here? Then yes. But why dinner and not breakfast?" Aurora wondered as she got up from the bed.

"Because it's more common for people to have dinner dates. Plus, a lot of people work during the day-time hours, so they have responsibilities to their jobs," Mirra explained as they left the room.

"Yes! I am very much excited to learn more about jobs. I hope that Ezra will give me one. It would be nice to feel like I am contributing…and, well, earning as well. It gives you independence, this job, doesn't it?"

"It can. Well, I think that money gives you independence more than anything. Depending on the job you take, sometimes the restrictions mean you can't travel, or you have to be at your desk a certain number of hours out of the day. In those cases, yes, you are independent, but you have restrictions depending on your job."

"Hmm, I'll have to be sure to tell Ezra that I am going to be traveling," Aurora said, already negotiating in her head.

"You learn quickly," Mirra laughed.

They walked through the back door of the guesthouse

and into the garden surrounded by lush palms. Luckily, the tables were empty of guests, though Aurora imagined it was a lovely spot to sit and watch the sun disappear into the water. Music played softly from somewhere, a light bouncy song, and string lights twinkled between the palms. The night held a soft breeze, and the moon had just begun its gentle rise over the water. Jolie stood by the edge of the ocean, staring out to the horizon, a red sarong wrapped loosely around her body.

"It's calm tonight," Jolie said when they stopped next to her. "The waves gentled just a bit ago as the moon came up."

"I don't know if my parents will still be around or not." Aurora shrugged one shoulder. "But I can try calling to them as well."

"That will likely help. I'm sure they are worried." Mirra squeezed her hand. "Shall we get on with it then?"

"Yes, I'd like to." Not just to try and find her parents and get this over with, Aurora thought, but because she hadn't been out of the water this long…ever. The ocean's heartbeat resonated with her own, calling to her, and she'd forever be tied to it. While she'd been enjoying her time on land, she was always conscious of the water calling to her.

Jolie glanced around to ensure the beach was empty before slipping off her sarong and walking naked into the water. Both Mirra and Aurora followed suit, and Aurora let out a sigh of relief when water swirled around her ankles. Now she understood why Mirra had explained that she would need to go into the ocean periodically to recharge. This was both the gift and the curse of their magick, and their powers needed careful tending.

Slipping beneath the surface, Aurora called forth her magick. It unfurled inside of her, a gentle glow that flowed through her limbs as she transformed. How would she explain a process like this to Nathan? It was something that was second nature to her, and she didn't know if she would have the words to explain how it felt. It just *was*.

Once her transformation was complete, Aurora rolled in the water, kicking experimentally to see if her fin would feel weird after being on two legs for a couple days. Her fin, a brilliant mix of shiny purples and turquoise blues, had particularly pretty markings. Though, in Aurora's opinion, all fins were beautiful – because each was unique.

The cool ocean water caressed her skin as she surged forward. For a moment, Aurora just luxuriated in the beauty of the ocean at night. Light from the moon filtered softly into the water, highlighting the reefs. Coral clustered with rocks, while sea fans rocked gently in the waves. An octopus, out on her nightly search for dinner, danced across the sand floor in a radiant display of colors. This was home, one which Aurora would always love, but even as they moved away from shore, she realized something.

She now also felt a pull to return to land.

Prior to coming here, Aurora had always held a strong desire to visit the islands. But she'd never felt a *pull* before. It was a want instead of a need. But as she swam further from land – from Nathan – Aurora understood what her heart had been trying to tell her.

Her home was in two places now.

It was an unnerving feeling, as all she'd ever known was the ocean, and Aurora understood that she would need time to process it all. That being said, she also understood herself well enough to know that she'd already made up her mind. One way or the other, she was going to figure out how to have a life on Siren Island – with Nathan – if he'd have her. She couldn't bring herself to consider his potential rejection, not with what she still had to face with her parents, so she pushed those thoughts aside and focused on the task at hand. Opening her mouth, Aurora pulled sound from her very soul – it was a special call – one known only between a child and its parents – and released her song to the ocean. The notes thundered through the water, startling a turtle who had hunkered down beneath a coral ledge for a sleep.

When her song was met with a response – Aurora closed her eyes – trying to figure out her emotions. While she was embarrassed for running away, she also was excited to see her parents. She hoped they could listen with open hearts and understand what she'd been trying to tell them for years.

Mirra and Jolie surprised her by linking their arms through hers, forming a trifecta, and together they powered through the water toward her parents. With their combined powers, the swim time was cut considerably shorter, and they met her parents in the dark abyss sooner than expected. Aurora stopped, not certain how to proceed.

"Aurora," Queen Madeline, her mother, made to rush forward but the king stopped her.

"You're safe, I see. Is it true you ran away from the guards?" King Donovan, otherwise known as her father, glowered at her. The similar feeling of being misunderstood and controlled roiled in her gut, making Aurora look up at him with sullen eyes.

"I did," Aurora said. Anger flashed across the king's face. Where once she would feel chastised, now Aurora straightened her shoulders. "I did because I've asked to go to land for a while now like the other Mer and you always refuse."

"But, darling, it's for your safety," Queen Madeline interjected. She clasped her hands in front of her, worry etched on her lovely face. They hovered in the inky depths, facing each other, and Aurora was certain their guards were near. "You're next in line to rule our village. There are a lot of dangers on land."

"And with mixing with humans," King Donovan added.

"Yes, but how would I govern our people if I'm not aware of those dangers? The world out there? Well, it changes – and changes fast. As a ruler, wouldn't you say it would be smart to be aware of those things? I think that I would be able to help our people..." Aurora paused for a moment to gather courage. "If I decide to rule at all."

"What!" Her father exploded, throwing his hands up, and swimming a few feet away in a frenzy. A shark, attracted by the frenetic motion, buzzed by them to see what the fuss was about. "What is this nonsense? Of course you will take the throne one day. You and your husband. That is the way of things."

"I don't know if that is what I want," Aurora said.

"You don't know? You don't know?" Her father repeated himself. "How can you not know? This is what you were born for. Do you know how many Mer wish to be in your position?"

"Perhaps you should interview one of them, then.

There might be better choices for the position of ruler. Did you know in the human world, they vote? Everyone votes?"

"A vote…" Her father's face grew thunderous.

"We do have votes, Aurora. You know that. Our advisors are all voted in. But you are the princess. What's happened to you?" Queen Madeline asked, confusion lacing her tone. "And who are these two that you've brought with you?"

"This is Mirra and Jolie," Aurora said, turning to the women who flanked her. "They live on Siren Island. On land. They run a successful business, they've found love with humans, and they've offered me a job. I don't want to return home."

"Shit…" Jolie muttered under her breath.

"A job?" King Donovan exploded again. "A job? What are you even talking about? Leave these women at once and come home where you belong."

"No," Aurora said, and Jolie swam a bit forward, placing herself between Aurora and the king.

"If I may?" Jolie asked and continued without waiting for a response. "I understand this must be quite difficult for you both to hear. And I think there probably needs to be some time to think things over. I don't believe that making a rash decision – either way – is what is best here. Aurora would like to spend some more time with us on Siren Island. We've grown up there, our mother is Irma."

"Irma! I know her," Queen Madeline exclaimed. "She's with the Mer from Australia now. The one who is looking to create a network for our tribes to connect with each other. It's fascinating, really."

"And clearly encouraging daughters of the Mer to run away…" King Donovan said.

"No, I'd never heard of them. I left because all of my friends go to land, and they tell me wonderful stories. I'm…I'm bored at home, don't you see? I want more. I want to learn about new and exciting things, to work, to meet new people," Aurora exclaimed in frustration. "I don't know if I want what you want for me."

"Your friends go to land?" The king looked to the queen who just shrugged.

"Yes, that is my point. The Mer are going to land whether you like it or not. The more you tell them not to go, the more they will try to go. It's why I left. I wanted to experience for myself. How will I know what the best choice for me is if I don't get to experience the options?" Aurora tried to explain herself.

"It's something we'd like to work on together," Jolie said, pointing to Aurora and Mirra. "We want to create a way to help the Mer that do want to visit, or stay, on land so that they are safe when they do so. There's a lot to learn about humans, and I completely understand why you're worried for Aurora's safety. I would be, too. I can promise you that we'll take care of her and protect her while she stays with us."

"Stays?" Queen Madeline's eyes widened.

"I propose you think about this for another few weeks. Spend some time speaking to your people and see just how many of them actually sneak away to visit the islands. Times are changing. Burying your head in the sand won't stop that. You know where Aurora is, so you won't have to worry. And Aurora can take some time to explore what life with humans is like. I think, once you both have more information, you can talk through this. What's important here is that you both acknowledge that you care about the other," Jolie said.

"I...well, of course I care about Aurora. That's why I'm so angry," King Donovan said. "A daughter's place is at home. With her family."

"Donovan," Queen Madeline stopped him with a touch to his arm. "Jolie is right. Let's give Aurora space to figure some things out on her own. If we hover over her and force her choices, how will she learn to be a good ruler? She needs to spend some time learning on her own. We need to talk to our people as well, and understand what is going on."

"Two weeks then – in human time." King Donovan surprised Aurora by swimming over and pressing a kiss to her forehead. "Don't do anything stupid. Make good choices. Be safe."

"I...I will," Aurora said, surprise filling her. "Thank you."

"I was so worried." This from her mother who now wrapped her arms around Aurora. "Don't do that again, please."

"I won't, I promise." Aurora realized that by sneaking away she'd caused pain for her parents, and she hadn't wanted to do that. Perhaps her choice had been childish, but she didn't regret the decision – just her execution of it.

"Please come and visit us to discuss this again in a fortnight. We have a place called The Laughing Mermaid and you are welcome there. You can even take a tour of the island if you like," Mirra said. "As our guests. We'll provide clothing and see to those details."

"An island tour? Well, that does sound interesting, I won't lie." Queen Madeline looked up at the king.

"We'll see. Aurora, be smart. We'll talk soon."

With that, her parents disappeared into the dark water, holding hands as they swam away. Aurora whirled on Jolie and grabbed her arms.

"You are a miracle-worker! A goddess!"

"I know, I know..." Jolie laughed. Hooking arms, they swam toward home.

CHAPTER 13

*N*athan was having a bad day.

Well, a distracted day. He'd run into more than one problem at work, and his team had stared at him over the video call, while he continued to trail off mid-sentence and stare into space. Finally, after his assistant had gently suggested they reconvene at a better time, he'd realized just how much Aurora was occupying his thoughts. It was as though nothing of import existed now that she was in his life. He'd be staring at the screen and his brain would dance over to thoughts of her in that silky dress and how her face lit up when she saw him.

Nobody had ever looked at him like that before. Like he was responsible for hanging the moon in the sky.

That thought had propelled him into trying something he rarely did – cooking. He'd had thoughts of having a romantic cooking session in the kitchen with Aurora, where they'd feed each other bits of their delicious concoctions while music played in the background. But, after he'd over-salted one dish and burned another, Nathan had admitted defeat and ordered take-out. It was best that he play to his strengths, and, well, cooking was not one of them. Now, with the fragrant scent of buttery Italian food wafting to him from the box on the back seat, Nathan pulled up at the Laughing Mermaid.

He'd decided to bring Aurora back to his house to spend time with her one-on-one there. It was important to him that they learn more about each other, and he thought he'd show her a little bit about his work. It seemed like she hadn't really understood what he did for a living, which wasn't surprising – most people didn't get the technicalities of it – but he found himself wanting to show her something he was proud of. Plus, if they did move to the next step in their relationship, he needed her to understand that sometimes he would spend long hours at the computer.

The next step.

His pulse raced as he thought about what would, or could, come next for them. Never before had someone impacted his life in such a way, and he winced thinking about just *how* many hours he did spend at the computer. Sure, work was a love for him. But did he need to be attached to his computer? Or was it something he did because he was used to being on his own?

Maybe that was why his ex-girlfriend had strayed. It wasn't the first time he'd thought this. She'd wanted to be out every night partying, and off on adventures during the day. While he liked to do that some of the time, his work demanded more of him. While she'd certainly enjoyed the lifestyle he could provide her – from a monetary standpoint – the reality of him actually having to work for it was a buzzkill for her. He'd have to make sure not to make the same mistake with Aurora and to give her the time and attention she deserved.

Like he could stop thinking about her anyway.

When the door opened and she stood there, beaming up at him, Nathan's brain froze. It was like when the sun came out from behind a cloud, the rays blinding his vision, and it took a moment for him to respond.

"I…every time I see you, I'm convinced you're the most beautiful woman in the world," Nathan said. Aurora's smile widened. She wore another silky dress that skimmed over her lush body, this one in a soft coral color that immediately made him think of her being naked. How was he going to think straight around her? Pulling his eyes up from her outfit, he leveled them on hers. He couldn't read anything but excitement in those pretty turquoise eyes of hers, and she genuinely seemed happy to see him. The nerves that had been locked in a tight ball inside him all day dissolved.

"I've missed you," Aurora said. She stepped forward and tilted her head up for a kiss, and Nathan's heart swelled.

He wanted this. *Her*. Every day of his life, Nathan wanted to see this face smiling at him, raising her lips for a kiss, and cuddling in next to him in bed. It didn't matter how long they'd known each other. Nathan had never been more certain of anything in his life. Now, he just had to figure out how to make her love him.

Love. It felt like love when her lips connected with his, the Laughing Mermaid dropping away behind them, his mind caught on how sweet she tasted. A little current of energy zipped through him at her touch, and once more

Nathan felt like he'd been plugged into an electrical socket.

"Ahem."

Nathan pulled back to see Jolie standing behind them, her arms crossed, an eyebrow raised.

"Hi Jolie."

"Hi Nathan. Have fun, you two lovebirds," Jolie said, closing the door behind them.

"Lovebird? Are there birds of love here?" Aurora tilted her head up to look at Nathan as they walked to his Jeep. He helped her into the car and then rounded the hood to get behind the steering wheel.

"Um, I don't believe so. Actually I don't really know the history behind where they live."

"But they are real?" Aurora asked. He pulled the Jeep back onto the street and soon the breeze was drifting through the car while the local reggae station played on the radio.

"They are. I believe they are called that because they have a strong bond. Once they mate – they are bonded for life."

"Really? That's so sweet. I don't know much about birds," Aurora admitted. "Is that common for a lot of birds?"

"I…I don't know," Nathan laughed, turning down his road. "I just know that this particular species got the name due to their devotion to their mate."

"I like that. It must be nice to be loved in such a way." Aurora's tone held a wistful note.

Don't tell her you love her. Don't tell her you love her. It's too soon.

Nathan pulled the Jeep to a stop and turned to Aurora.

"You deserve to be loved in such a way." When the smile bloomed on her face, Nathan figured he'd said the right thing without throwing himself at her feet.

Once he'd collected the food from the back, they went inside to the villa. Nerves returned, and Nathan searched for something to talk about that wouldn't make him sound awkward. He hated when he got stuck like this, and he would return to silence in lieu of sounding stupid.

Luckily, Aurora left him little time to feel stuck. Already she was chattering away about what she'd learned the day before – asking him something about hot girl summers.

"Wait, what are you talking about?" Nathan finally tuned into the conversation. "A hot girl summer?"

"Yes, I read it in a magazine. Apparently it's a whole thing. Girls go out of their way to have a hot girl summer. I guess it means you're meant to dress extra nice. Because, well, isn't summer mostly hot anyway? Well, winter is, too, here, isn't it? So, how do you have a hot girl summer if it is already hot outside?"

"Or if you're always hot?" Nathan said, running a finger down her arm and giving her a slow smile.

"I'm quite comfortable most of the time," Aurora said, squinting at him in confusion.

"Um, no, hot can mean beautiful. Sexy. Pretty," Nathan explained, now realizing that Aurora didn't quite get the meaning of the slang word. That was interesting. Even though she'd grown up sheltered, how was it that term hadn't made its way to her island?

"Ohhhhhh," Aurora drew the word out, laughing at herself.

"I hope you're hungry," Nathan said, quickly changing the subject so she wouldn't feel embarrassed. There was no reason to be embarrassed over something she hadn't learned yet, but he wanted to protect her feelings.

"I am. I was promised dinner," Aurora smiled at him.

"Can I get you a glass of wine?" Nathan held up a bottle of red and Aurora nodded. She trailed her hand across the countertop, watching him with interest as he opened the bottle and poured them both a glass. She seemed particularly fascinated by the microwave, and he wondered what caused her to be so transfixed.

"I was thinking we'd eat on the deck. We can watch the rest of the sunset from there."

"Perfect, how can I help?" Aurora asked.

"Just by being you…" Nathan dropped a quick kiss on her lips. Though he wanted to linger, he knew he should take it slow. There was no way to know if Aurora would be scared off if he started talking about a future together. Picking up the food, he carried it through the sliding glass doors to where he'd set the outdoor table. Earlier today, he'd taken time to walk around his garden and cut flowers from the tropical bushes and had stuffed them in vases and jam jars. While maybe he wasn't the most artistic with flower design, he found them to be cheerful and hoped Aurora would think so, too. He'd scattered the vases around the deck floor, on the railing, and on the table. Then, he'd strung up the twinkle lights he'd had sitting in a box on the kitchen counter for weeks. He dropped the food on the table and grabbed the lighter he'd left out and lit the tiki torches that lined the deck railings. Finally, he turned and found Aurora smiling up at him.

"This is just so lovely. Did you put all these flowers together for me?"

"I was trying to make a pretty spot for dinner since we weren't going out to a restaurant," Nathan explained.

Aurora walked to him and wound her arms around his waist. Leaning in, she turned, so that she could look at the deck, and the sun hanging low over the ocean just past it. Two gulls swooped lazily overhead, pretending nonchalance, their keen eyes having spotted Nathan's food bags. They stood like this for a moment, quietly absorbing the beauty, and Nathan could have sworn he felt a warm hum of energy pass between them. It was one of those perfect moments, and he knew it would forever be etched in his brain.

The moment drew out into an hour. They lingered over the meal – eggplant parmesan, vegetarian lasagna, and decadent crusts of garlic bread – and another bottle of wine.

"Tell me more about what work is like for you. I can't say that I really understand it," Aurora said, gesturing with the glass of wine in her hand. Her cheeks had taken on a rosy glow, but Nathan didn't think her to be all that tipsy. She clearly could hold her alcohol, which was another point in her favor. Hell, who was he kidding? She was already off the scale with the number of points she'd racked up. He couldn't remember the last time he'd had long conversations with someone without stumbling over his words or searching for topics to discuss. It was freeing, being with her, and he relished the feeling of not having social anxiety as a stumbling block. Now, though, he hoped she wouldn't think he was too nerdy as he launched into an explanation of his work.

"Okay, so I told you that I design video games, right? I can understand where it gets confusing because I actually straddle several types of work in what I do."

"Tell me more," Aurora said, leaning in, and Nathan tried not to be distracted by the way her lovely breasts shifted under the almost-nude silk of her dress. His bracelet shimmered at her wrist, and it felt good to see her wearing something he'd given her.

"I'm both a programmer and a designer. I have more people who make up my team who actually do one or the other in those roles, but I straddle both, because, well – when I had my game idea, I wanted to be able to execute in both areas. I ended up taking extra courses to learn, but it's been really beneficial to me."

Aurora nodded, and he hoped he wasn't boring her.

"See, a programmer will do all the coding and the behind-the-scenes stuff – like what actually makes the video game run. It's super involved and technical, but it's sort of the command system that drives the characters in the game. The designer side will create how they want things to look. How the characters move. What the colors are. What the overarching story of the world is. Yeah, it's more world-building and bringing a vision to life. I wanted a hand in both, but my team helps bring it to life as much as I do," Nathan finished.

Aurora just stared at him, and Nathan flushed, realizing he was probably boring her.

"And your team? Where are they?" Aurora asked, looking at the villa.

"Oh, so I work with people from all over the world. We communicate online or on calls. It's great because we can work in our comfort zones and at our speed, but then we also will have sessions where we collaborate together."

"On your phone! You take calls on that." Aurora nodded her head vigorously and Nathan, again, found her response just a touch odd. But, nevertheless, he smiled at her.

"Yes, we do have a lot of calls. I think, maybe…should I just show you what I create? Would you like to see my game?"

A look of relief flashed across Aurora's face for an instant before she smiled at him. Maybe he was boring her with his work talk, but he didn't really blame her. Not everyone was going to find what he did interesting, and that was just fine with him.

"I'd love to," Aurora said.

"Let me just clean up first so we don't get any scavengers after the leftovers," Nathan said, nodding to the gulls. Aurora stood to help, and in a few moments they had the food packed away inside and Nathan had topped off her wine glass.

"This is where you work?" Aurora had seen the space briefly the other night on the way to the bedroom, but now Nathan flicked on all the lights to showcase his office. He had three desks that created kind of a half-circle, with one of the desks allowing him to stand when he was feeling antsy from sitting too long. With four monitors, several keyboards, and various tablets for hand drawing and design, it was an impressive set-up. He'd been surprised he'd managed to pack it all and get it here safely but was happy he'd been able to do so. It allowed him to work in the way that he preferred.

"Poseidon's Crusade?" Aurora read, looking at the posters of his video game he'd taped to the walls. Her mouth hung open as she studied the underwater scenes, taking in all of the various characters he'd created, as well as the mermaid art from the shop downtown. She stood, frozen in one spot, and Nathan went to her.

"Yeah, that's the name of my game. Would you like to see?" Nathan rubbed his hands up and down her arms, confused at her reaction.

"Please show me," Aurora said, an odd note in her voice.

Though he was unsure of her reaction, Nathan took her at her word. Pulling out a chair from the corner of his office, he set it next to his and gestured for her to sit. Maybe playing the game would help? He handed her a controller and she just gaped down at it.

"What is this?" Aurora asked.

"It's a video game controller. See the arrows?" Nathan gave her a quick tutorial in how to use the controller and she bit her lower lip as she listened intently. Worried at her reaction – usually she asked a million questions – he hesitated before turning the console on.

"Do you want to play the game? We can do something else, too."

"No, I want to see this. Please," Aurora added.

"Okay, so basically the point of the game is twofold – build your village and defend it against attacks." Nathan flipped the console on, firing up his screens, and Aurora gasped as the screens boomed to life with the opening credit for his video game. He let the intro roll, a two-minute animated movie that brought to life his characters and their mission. Aurora gasped again as his mermaid, Serena, swam into view and began speaking.

"Your mission, should you choose to accept it, is to find me my king so that we may build our kingdom together." Serena spoke, twirling in the water as she did so.

"A mermaid…" Aurora whispered.

"Do you like mermaids?" Nathan asked, glancing over at her.

"I love them." Aurora's tone was almost reverent as she stared at the screen, transfixed by the video. "Is this… is this a movie?"

"Um, yes, a short, animated movie."

"The girls were telling me about these…" Aurora said, so softly that he almost didn't catch it. That was also odd – had she really never heard of movies before? How was that even possible?

"Okay, it's go time. So you'll pick up your controller and pick your player…"

"Can I be the mermaid?" Aurora asked immediately.

"Of course you can. She's a very popular character," Nathan said, grinning at her. Aurora looked strikingly similar to Serena, and even more so now that he could compare the two closely. It was like Serena had walked out of his video game and into real life. Amused by his thoughts, Nathan returned to explaining the game.

"Okay, I'm going to be a warrior. My job is going to be to protect you as you build your village."

"Oh look!" Aurora exclaimed as the opening scene moved into the underwater world. Serena hovered in the water, waiting for direction, while a school of silver fish swam past. Nathan pushed the buttons on his controller so that his warrior swam up to Serena.

"You can move her to start the game..." Nathan pointed to Aurora's controller. She jabbed a few buttons, sending Serena in an awkward circle in the water, and Aurora gasped.

"Did I just do that?"

"Yes, you did." Amused, Nathan sent his warrior in a circle around Serena, holding up his controller so that Aurora could see how he was manipulating his player. A quick study, Aurora soon had Serena blasting through the ocean and off on her adventure.

"What!" Aurora exclaimed, an hour later, completely engrossed in the game. "That would never happen. Sharks don't attack in that way. They're really quite precious."

"I don't know that I've ever heard a shark referred to as precious before..." Nathan cocked his head at her. He'd long since stopped truly playing, instead letting her explore his game, her absorption in his work so complete that he wasn't sure she even heard the things she was saying.

But her words were...out there. Like...Nathan was having a hard time accepting what he was hearing from her, because if these were really her thoughts, then Aurora wasn't really living in this reality.

Instead of her just being a quirky and sheltered island girl, now Nathan wondered if she needed help. Because, well...

Poseidon would never do that. His magick comes from the heart of the ocean.

Turtles will tell you if there is danger.

Most Mer won't ever attack unless threatened.

Sirens will actually sing to warn of danger, not to entice men.

Mer can swim faster than sharks.

It's much harder for Mer to have babies than you think. Populating a kingdom would take far longer than you realize.

"They are though! They keep the reefs healthy. Sharks are very misunderstood. They need us to love them, not be afraid of them. I'm always happy when I see my shark friends," Aurora said, her eyes glued to the screen. Nathan's thoughts whirled as the level ended and Aurora sat back with a delighted sigh. Turning to him, she dropped her controller and launched herself into his lap, winding her arms around his neck as he caught her while trying to stop the chair from tipping over.

"Nathan! You *do* believe in mermaids," Aurora exclaimed, and then her lips were on his before he could muster a response.

CHAPTER 14

*T*he video game had been an absolute revelation for Aurora. Playing it had crumbled the last of the reservations she held regarding Nathan, and now she knew that not only did she love him, she could be truthful with him about who she was. Aurora didn't like hiding this part of herself from him, and she'd known when he'd picked her up from the Laughing Mermaid and her heart had danced in her chest that this was love. Maybe it didn't make sense, or maybe it did, but Aurora didn't care. She just knew one thing – Nathan had been adamant about trust being important in a relationship. Before they took any steps further, she needed to show him just who she was. It was the right thing to do.

Breaking the kiss, she cradled his face in her palms. Already, she could feel his need for her growing beneath her lap, and a long liquid pull of lust slipped through her. She shivered, wanting him more than anything, but knew she needed to do the right thing first. Aurora slid off his lap and stood, holding out her hands.

"Will you come with me? I have something to show you."

"Aurora...I...is everything all right?" Nathan asked. Worry danced behind his eyes, and warmth bloomed in her that he genuinely cared about her feelings.

"Of course, I'm just so excited to see your work. It shows me that...well, that you get it. That you understand. You're a friend to my people, you see?" Aurora chattered, dragging Nathan down the steps and into the main room of the villa.

"Your people? Like the islanders at Triste?" Nathan asked, confusion lacing his voice.

"No, that's not what I mean. But I'm ready to show you now." Aurora pulled Nathan so that they stood on the side of the pool outside his villa. A lovely blue light lit it from within, and the water looked clean and inviting. All Aurora needed was water to change into her Mer form.

"Aurora...are you okay?" Nathan asked, again. He brought his hands to her shoulders and searched her eyes. She saw concern there and realized that he probably thought she was acting odd. Well, she was, wasn't she? She'd all but lost herself in the mermaid game, and then dragged him downstairs mumbling about showing him something. She'd better just show him now before she lost her confidence.

"I am well. I just...Nathan, I need to show you something. Something very private to me and I'm asking that you honor me with keeping what happens here between just us. You...you told me that trust is very important to you in a relationship." Nerves made her stomach twist as she looked up at him, the reflection of the light from the pool rippling over his face.

"It is, very much so," Nathan agreed. She put a finger to his lips to stop him from saying more.

"I hope you'll understand why I've kept this from you. And maybe it will explain why I don't always understand things here. But first I have to ask for your promise that you'll protect my secret."

"I promise," Nathan said immediately, and Aurora believed him.

"I also want to tell you something…" Aurora sucked in a breath and blew it out before rushing forward, "I love you. I know it seems unusual or rushed but I need you to hear this."

"Aurora," Nathan began, his face lighting with joy.

"No, please, don't say it back…not yet…" Aurora held her finger to his lips again. "If what you feel is the same, I need you to say it when you know me. All of me."

"Okay?" Nathan drew out the last word, a cautious look slipping onto his face.

"Please just let me…" Aurora went to step back, but Nathan caught her to him, wrapping his arms around her in a warm hug. She leaned in, immediately soothed by his presence, and inhaled his clean scent. Tilting her chin up, she accepted his kiss, enjoying the hum of pleasure that zipped between them.

"You can't just tell me you love me and then step away," Nathan said against her lips.

"I'm sorry. I'm nervous."

"I can feel that. You're safe with me, Aurora. I'm ready to hear what you need to share." With one final kiss,

Nathan stepped back and waited. Aurora took a deep breath, and blew it out, allowing his words to calm her.

"It's…" Aurora shook her head with a laugh. How did one even begin? Perhaps it just made sense to show him. She grabbed the hem of her dress and pulled it over her head and dropped it across the back of a chair. Toeing off her sandals, she walked back to the side of the pool, comfortable in her nakedness.

Nathan, however, stood frozen with his mouth open as he gaped at her.

Aurora looked down at herself and then back up at him, wondering if perhaps the change to her mermaid form might be too much for him if her naked body was bringing out such a response.

"You're incredible…" Nathan breathed, and Aurora realized he was just staring at her with lust. A look down his body at his physical reaction affirmed her belief.

"Well, if you think this is incredible…just wait." Aurora dove neatly into the pool. The water slipped around her, cool against her skin, and she rose to the top to break the surface.

"I wish I could come in there with you," Nathan said, longing in his gaze. He crouched on the side of the pool, watching her.

"Nathan," Aurora's voice caught. "I'd like to show you who I really am."

With that, she sunk beneath the surface and called upon her magick, completing her transformation as quickly as she could. She stayed at the bottom a moment after she'd finished, anxiety kicking in, as she was nervous to see his face.

A splash sounded, and Aurora turned, gasping as she saw Nathan sink into the pool. His arms flailed in unnatural movements against the water, causing him to sink further, his eyes wide as he tried to reach her. Aurora was by his side instantly, and circling an arm around his waist, she brought him to the surface quickly.

"Oh my god," Nathan gasped, coughing, his entire body vibrating with shock and adrenaline. He heaved again, shaking, as she swam him to the shallow side of the pool where he could sit on a ledge. Once Nathan found his feet, he grasped the side of the pool, visibly shaking as he gulped for air. His glasses were gone, and his eyes stretched wide in his face.

"I thought you'd drowned," Nathan gasped out, holding a hand to his chest.

"Is that why you dove in the pool?" Aurora asked. "But you can't even swim."

"I didn't know...you were under for so long..." Nathan said, gasping for air.

"But...Nathan. I'm Mer. This is me. I can breathe under water," Aurora said carefully.

Nathan gulped and nodded vigorously, his hand still at his chest, very clearly shaken.

"That makes sense now, yes. Well, nothing makes sense. But yes, it would make sense that a mermaid could breathe under water, but I didn't really get that you were... or what was happening and then you were under water... and now you're here...a mermaid...shit, I'm babbling like a lunatic." Nathan grimaced, trying to slow his breathing, and Aurora understood she'd gone about this all wrong. Clearly, she'd terrified the man. However, the fact that he'd seen her change and still had tried to rescue her clarified her path for her. Nathan was the one for her, if she could talk him back from the panic that seemed to be creeping over him.

"Will you come closer?" Aurora asked. She could only swim so far to him and since he was in the shallows, she'd just be speaking to his kneecaps then. Nathan automatically complied, grasping the edge of the pool like a lifeline, and walked until the water hit his chest. Sensing he could go no further, Aurora swam close and reached out a hand to touch his chest. "May I hug you?"

"Yes," Nathan sputtered, his body still shaking with adrenaline.

Aurora wrapped her arms around his waist, and his automatically came around her. They stood there for what seemed like ages, the night stars sparkling above them, until Nathan's shivering subsided. Finally, he spoke.

"This is real." It wasn't a question.

"This is real, Nathan. I'm Mer. Mermaids actually exist, quite a lot of them in tribes around the world."

"Oh, hell, there's more of you? I...I just...this is..."

"Of course there's more of us," Aurora laughed. "I didn't just hatch from an egg."

"I have no idea how it works," Nathan said. "Just... ugh, I wish I could see better..."

"Hold on." Aurora turned and dove beneath the water, retrieving his glasses from the floor of the pool. Once he'd secured them back over his eyes, he just gaped at her.

"Can I...can I touch it?"

"My fin?" Aurora asked. "Of course."

She twisted so that Nathan could run a hand down her fin, shivering at his touch, as he marveled at her.

"Aurora, you're so beautiful. This fin…it's incredible. And soft to the touch. I wasn't expecting that, not really. I guess I wasn't sure what to expect." Nathan ran a hand through his hair, a giddy expression on his face. "I don't even know how to process this. It's mind-blowing. It shouldn't be real. But it is! Have I drank too much? Is this some joke you are playing on me?"

"It's no joke. It's just me," Aurora said, quietly. She pulled at her magic, dipping under the water once more, and changed back to her human form. Then, surfacing, she stood on the pool floor and walked to him.

"Oh. My. God." Nathan just shook his head. "How does it work? I can't understand…I need all the details."

"It's magick," Aurora said, shrugging it off as no big deal.

"We don't have magick in our world, Aurora," Nathan said, as Aurora pressed herself against him once more. Looking up, she rested her chin on his chest.

"Sure you do. You just have to look for it," Aurora said.

"I am honestly so overwhelmed right now. I don't even know how to respond – please tell me if I say anything insulting. Truly, I don't mean to be. I just, my brain is exploding. This is just…you're incredible. This is incredible. Mermaids are real! Like…it's like I called you to life in my video game. I just…"

"It's why I told you, actually. Once I saw your game, I realized that you might be accepting of who I am," Aurora's voice trembled.

At that, Nathan stilled, hearing the catch in her voice. Slowly, he brought both hands to her face, cradling it as though she was the most precious being in the world. Ever so gently, he brushed a kiss across her lips.

"Aurora. I do. I accept who you are. It's blowing my mind right now, and I'll have a thousand questions for you, but please know it is only out of shock and excitement. It's not because I don't love you."

"You love me?" Aurora asked, hope shivering in her heart. "Even after seeing this?"

"Even *more* after seeing this. How could I not? You're a goddess. A magickal goddess of the ocean and land and you've forever enchanted me," Nathan said against her lips. Aurora's heart broke open and love rushed through her. Now, she was desperate with need and she all but clawed her way up Nathan's body, wrapping her legs around his waist, as she sucked desperately at his bottom lip.

"I need you," Aurora whimpered against his lips.

"And I you…" Nathan gasped. "Just…let me… water…" He stumbled a bit as he worked his way along the side of the pool and up the wide shallow steps. Aurora shivered as the night air hit her wet body, but still Nathan held her, walking her toward a double lounge chair. There, he nudged her legs so that she slid down his body. She moaned as she came in contact with his hard length, and he stilled when she ran a hand over him.

"I want to kiss you here," Aurora said, sitting on the lounge so her face was at his waist. "Like you did to me the other night."

"I won't stop you." Nathan's hips jerked forward when

she reached over and undid his shorts, sliding them, along with his underwear, down his legs. Slowly she ran a finger over his length, enjoying the silky smoothness of his skin, before leaning over to lick experimentally at his length. When his hips jerked again, and a small moan left his lips, she figured she was doing something right. And much like anything in Aurora's life, she jumped in with enthusiasm.

Taking him deep in her mouth, she moaned herself as she licked the length of him, sucking gently and kissing along his hardness. This was a lot of fun, Aurora realized, as liquid heat tugged low in her body, and she squirmed against the cushion. The soft breeze caressed her skin, and the sounds of the waves hitting the beach far below them filled the night.

"Wait, wait…" Nathan pulled back, gasping lightly. "If you keep going, I won't last and I want to last."

"I like doing that…a lot. Did you enjoy it?" Aurora looked up at him, licking her lips where she could still taste him. She wanted to devour this man, and her body ached for his touch. She scooted backwards on the lounge, opening her legs and beckoned to him with one finger.

"It felt amazing, Aurora." Nathan dropped to his knees between her legs and before she could respond, his mouth was at her breasts, teasing her sensitive nipples before he dropped lower, kissing where she wanted him most. Aurora arched against his mouth, pleasure shooting straight through her, as he lapped languidly. Liquid heat built, and when he slid a finger inside of her, she exploded, bucking against him as waves of lust consumed her.

Before he could stop, Aurora pulled him up and over her, linking her arms over her shoulders as she looked up at him. He'd lost his glasses somewhere along the way again, and now moonlight glimmered in his eyes.

"I want you. All of you," Aurora said.

"I just have to ask…what do you do for protection?" Nathan held still, waiting for her response.

"Protection?"

"Against getting pregnant. Babies. I don't even know how that works with Mer…" Nathan trailed off and shook his head.

"Oh, of course. We don't have protection. Babies are a gift in our world as they are difficult to conceive," Aurora explained.

"We…humans have an option for protection. It's called a condom. I can go get one and then we wouldn't risk a child. I need to know what you want me to do before we go any further," Nathan explained patiently, though he continued to rub his length against her, causing her hips to rock with his. She wanted to feel him. All of him. Deep inside of her.

"I want your babies. It's highly unlikely we'd conceive. It usually takes a lot of times for a mermaid to become with child. But what do you want?" Aurora bit her lip, realizing they had so much to figure out still.

"I'd have a hundred babies with you, Aurora." Nathan's tone was serious, and she knew that he meant it. They'd already spoken of their desire for family in the past.

"In that case, no – please don't stop. You're making me…I just…I want…" Aurora felt she was dangerously close to whining, and Nathan grinned, his lips at her neck.

He bit lightly, the pain surprising her, and he slid deep inside of her, filling her.

It was like nothing she'd ever experienced before. She'd thought she'd known love? Her past lovers were not it. This was...something *so* much more. Emotion consumed Aurora as Nathan drove into her repeatedly, his hardness filling her slick softness. Heat built, and Nathan's lips found hers.

"I love you, my beautiful mermaid," Nathan said, relentlessly plunging into her. The press of his weight, the heat of his body, the repeated thrusts over and over pulled her right to the edge. But his words? They tumbled her right over. She clenched around him, exploding with lust, as he groaned against her lips finding his own release.

"I love you, too," Aurora said, threading her arms around him and looking over her shoulder at the stars above them.

You wish upon stars in the human world, Mirra had told her.

So, Aurora picked a star and sent her wish to the heavens.

CHAPTER 15

*T*he next week became a blur of highs and lows for Aurora. The highs including spending every available moment with Nathan, learning all his interesting quirks, and discovering how to pleasure each other as lovers. The lows only came in those moments where Aurora let her mind drift to how she was going to make this relationship work in the long term. She loved Nathan, fiercely and without reservations, but the weight of responsibility hung heavy on her shoulders when it came to the future of her people. Sure, she'd been flippant when she'd told her father to get someone else to run the village. The reality was, however, that it would take years of training to get the suitable person in place. Training which she'd been given since she was little.

Maybe there was a new way to do things, Aurora kept telling herself. Just because the training and protocols had always been done one way didn't mean it had to be done the same in the future. Because right now? It felt like she was stuck between an impossible choice – choose her people or choose herself.

She wrapped a sarong around herself and smiled at Nathan as he came into the kitchen. Aurora had started to learn his patterns of work, understanding that there were times he couldn't be interrupted. She'd been doing her own work, making notes about observations that would be helpful for Jolie's course, and trying to document all the questions she had about living on land. It felt good to be productive, as though she was making a difference, and Aurora found that she enjoyed working in something different than training to be a ruler.

"I'm kind of nervous about you going tonight," Nathan said. He crossed the room and wrapped his arms around her waist, hugging Aurora against his broad chest. It was one of her favorite things about him – his hugs – and she leaned into his warmth.

"Why?" Aurora asked.

"Because what if something happens? I can't help you. What if you don't come back?" Nathan's voice rumbled in his chest against her ear, and she tightened her hold.

"It's safer for me in the water than it is on land," Aurora said. "Nothing threatens me in the ocean."

"But what if your parents come and steal you back?" Nathan asked.

"They won't." Surprised, Aurora pulled back to look up at him. "They gave their word. My parents are very honorable."

"I don't want to lose you, Aurora." Nathan bent and teased her lips with a kiss. Several times this week he'd brought up questions about what their future could look like, and she hadn't been able to give him an answer that was satisfactory. Nathan was a planner, and he was very regimented when it came to certain things. He couldn't yet see how he would fit into her life, and that worried him. Aurora wished she could say something to assuage his concerns, but she didn't have an answer. Yet.

"I don't want to lose you either, Nathan. But the reality is we come from two different worlds. There may be times where we have to be apart. I don't know what that will look like yet, but we'll figure it out. Together."

Nathan ran his hands up and down her back, soothing her as much as himself, and they said no more. What was there to say? A good solution hadn't presented itself yet.

Nathan carried his laptop out to the deck, wanting to be close while she went for a night swim. She found it adorable that he worried for her, but the ocean wasn't a threat. It made sense that he worried, as he couldn't swim, so the sea must seem like a very big and scary place to him. But to her? It was home. Although, he had been taking copious notes this week about her experience living underwater. She'd spent more time playing his game with him, pointing out where he'd gotten things wrong, and giving him ideas on what he could add. That had really made her feel good. Not only had he listened to her suggestions, but he'd engaged her in heated debates about particular points of design and game strategy. It had proven to be quite fun, arguing with someone for the sake of debate, and it was even more fun when Nathan bent her over the desk during one particularly heated debate. Aurora had decided then and there to try and provoke Nathan on occasion as the results were quite stimulating.

Aurora took the steps that led from the deck to the sandy beach. She'd waited until almost midnight before deciding to go to the water, as Nathan lived on a busier stretch of the beach. This was how her life would be though – her needing to get into the water and transform every few days no matter what. She'd always be looking over her shoulder and trying to hide what she was from people. It wasn't always the easiest, the girls had explained, but it could be done. Maybe Nathan would be willing to move to a more private location? Or Mirra had pointed out she could just drive to another part of the island and enter the ocean from there. That part didn't seem to bring the women much stress, so Aurora wasn't going to worry about it.

Slipping off her sarong, she dove quickly beneath the surface and didn't come back up lest someone was looking from their windows. She swam through the undertow and the tumble of waves that surged at the shoreline and continued past the shallow reef where a lobster raced out of his hole to greet her, spiny antennas waving in front of him. She smiled, waggling her fingers at it, and allowed her magick to flow through her to complete her trans-formation.

Once she was in Mer form, Aurora lingered for a moment, hovering in the water over the reef. It felt good to change – it always did – but she wanted to feel if anything else had changed. She immediately noticed the pull she felt toward land – toward Nathan – that echoed how she had felt last week when she'd gone to meet her parents. The feeling of being split between two homes – two worlds – was new, but not unwelcome. However, she'd never been in love before, not truly, so Aurora wanted to take some time to assess her feelings in a space where she felt safe.

Aurora twirled onto her back, looking up at the moon through the surface, the water making the glowing orb ripple and shift. She was the happiest she'd ever been, while still being the most anxious. This anxiety thing was new to her – as it wasn't a feeling she'd experienced in the Mer world. There had been nothing to be anxious about in her old life. She was safe, the village was happy, and life followed a routine. Yes, she'd been bored and itching for more – but that hadn't brought anxiety. She hadn't even realized that she could be someone who was prone to worrying, and Aurora found she didn't particularly enjoy it. Taking action was more her style, but there wasn't anything she could do in this moment to change the decisions that would be made in the future. Her parents could demand she return home, and if she refused, she'd lose them.

Aurora floated, tuning into her emotions, and soon she realized that she felt different. She couldn't quite put her finger on it, but maybe it was just that she'd grown as a person – and a woman – very quickly in such a short time. It had been a time of rapid growth, from meeting Nathan to taking on a job, and there was still so much to learn about life on land. Whether her parents would ever be able to acknowledge it or not, Aurora was a changed woman.

"Aurora."

Aurora whirled at the voice, startled to have her ruminations interrupted.

"Oracle." Aurora immediately bowed her head.

A soft glow surrounded the Oracle, her eyes white in

her loving face, a gentle smile on her lips. She was much revered among the Mer though most would only speak with her once in their lifetime. Aurora had been given a reading on her eighteenth birthday, one which had left her with more confusion than answers, and she hadn't expected another meeting for a long time. Often, rulers would meet with the Oracle from time to time if the Mer had a moment of crisis, but it wasn't a regular occurrence.

"It's been almost a decade since we last spoke," the Oracle said. Her smile widened, as though pleased with what she saw in Aurora. "You look well."

"Thank you, Oracle. I'm both well and unwell, if that's to be believed." Aurora swam closer, away from the curious looks of the fish clustered around the reef, and the Oracle drifted with her into deeper water.

"I can sense that about you," the Oracle said. "Would you like to talk about it?"

"Talk?" Aurora stuttered. She'd never heard of anyone having an actual discussion with the Oracle. Usually, the Mer were meant to keep their mouths shut and listen so as not to miss a single word the Oracle said.

"I do, from time to time, partake in conversations." The Oracle's voice held an amused note.

"I wouldn't want to disrespect your valuable time with my issues," Aurora protested.

"My time is my own to decide how to use," the Oracle said simply.

"Of course. Um, well, the quick version? I feel stifled living in my village. I want more from my life. I ran away from home and fell in love with a human who can't even swim and my parents expect me to return home in a few days."

"And what is the most important part of all of that?" The Oracle asked.

"I…" Aurora paused as they swam lazily through the sea. "Love. I would say that love is the most important part of that."

"But your parents love you as well," the Oracle challenged.

"Yes but…that's different." As soon as she said it, Aurora realized the truth of the matter. It was different. Parental love was one thing, but finding a partner – true love – well, that was something else entirely. Different kinds of love, both important in their own right. And, ultimately, it shouldn't have to be on her to pick one or the other.

"It is," the Oracle acknowledged. "The love of family is much different than that of a partner. Sometimes, familial love…it comes with burdens. Pressure. Projections. The parents project the future for their child that they determine to be the best. But the child, well, the woman, should know her own mind to go forth and make decisions for her future as she sees fit."

"I know what I want," Aurora admitted. She ran a finger over the bracelet that Nathan had given her. "But I don't know if I can have it."

"This is a good man?"

"He is, yes. And he's enthused about me being Mer and wants to protect me."

"You were born to be a changemaker, Aurora. For your people." The Oracle stopped, floating in the water, and turned to Aurora. Her white eyes scanned Aurora's body. "How you choose to enact that change is on you."

"YOU'RE SAYING that I should go for love and not worry about my family? What about my people and my responsibility to rule?" Aurora felt dangerously close to whining.

"Being a changemaker is rarely a comfortable role, Aurora. Nevertheless, they are needed in order to move our world forward." The Oracle pressed her lips together and waited.

"So...my people need me," Aurora said, her heart falling.

"They do." The Oracle studied her, an odd look on her face, as though she was waiting for Aurora to figure something out.

"I can't be a ruler while living on land."

"Likely not, no," the Oracle agreed, bowing her head in agreement.

"So it's back to one or the other...and I guess, you're saying I have to do what's best for me." Aurora searched the Oracle's face for signs.

"And for your pregnancy." The Oracle's words ripped Aurora's heart open, and she gaped at the other Mer.

"Did you...are you..." Panic mixed with excitement, and Aurora brought her hand to her stomach.

"You can't say you didn't know?"

"It's...I mean...I thought I felt a bit different, but I'm very emotional right now about my personal situation. Isn't it too soon to know?" Aurora asked.

"No, it's not too soon. You know the Mer are able to know almost instantly when conception occurs."

"How can I be sure?" Aurora whispered.

"Use your magick. Close your eyes and go inside yourself. Is it just you anymore?" The Oracle's voice was soothing the edge of her nerves, which Aurora greatly appreciated, as her mind whirled with conflicting thoughts.

Closing her eyes, she followed her magick, visualizing it flowing through her body in a lovely pink-hued glow. She sent it out on a mission, and it flowed through her, coming to surround a small, but powerful, light in her womb. Tears filled her eyes as she realized this light wasn't her own, but that of her baby. A miracle.

"You're right," Aurora gasped, opening her eyes to find the Oracle beaming at her.

"I know," the Oracle shrugged a shoulder.

"I mean, of course you are, you're the Oracle and all. Oh…Goddess, what am I going to do? A baby! I've always wanted one, but this just…I feel like I don't know what to do. If my parents learn about the pregnancy they'll insist that I return home and likely put me under lock and key. Nathan would never see his child." The last thought caused her stomach to twist.

"Maybe if you go to them of your own accord, you can work this out together."

"And Nathan? Will I tell him that I have to go home, or do I speak with him first about the baby?" Aurora rubbed her hand in a circular motion over her stomach, unsure of what to do.

"That I cannot say. You have choices to make. You are loved, Aurora. That's a very powerful thing to have. But your decisions are your own to make. I can only guide you insofar as to say this as a reminder – you always have a choice. Do not let others dictate your path for you." The Oracle touched her heart. "Listen here first."

With that, the Oracle swam over and pressed a kiss to Aurora's brow, before disappearing into the dark depths. Aurora turned, following the pull to shore, where Nathan waited patiently for her on the deck of his villa.

She didn't know if she should tell him right away or take a moment to think about what the baby would mean for her family. Would this change everything? It was a stupid question, of course it would. Her parents might have grown accustomed to the idea of sharing Aurora with Nathan, but that kind of adjustment took time. As soon as they knew about the baby, Aurora imagined they'd bring the full force of their influence upon her to make her stay in their kingdom.

Finding the little ball of light in her womb once more, she held her hand to her skin as she swam.

"Don't worry, little one. You will always be loved. This much, I promise you."

CHAPTER 16

*S*omething was off with Aurora.

Nathan didn't know how he knew it, but already he felt so in tune with her, that he could tell something was bothering her. Her once enthusiastic and joyful approach to discovering the island had dimmed, and now she asked to stay in the villa and relax, instead of going for the cave exploration that he had previously planned for today. Happy to acquiesce, Nathan had set up a lounger under a shady umbrella and had gone out to pick up brunch from Lola's.

"How's the love life?" Lola asked as she packed up his food. It was busier in the shop today, so Nathan didn't want to give too many details.

"Perfect. Beyond…she's, well, she's amazing," Nathan admitted, feeling warmth slip through him as he talked about Aurora. His woman.

His mermaid.

"Do I know this lovely lady?" Lola arched a brow at him, and Nathan shook his head. It was a small island, so it wasn't uncommon for people to know each other, but the coconut telegraph was strong here. If he'd been dating a local, the news would be all over the island within the day.

"Her name is Aurora. She's from Triste Islands and visiting…for now."

Lola's hands stilled as her head came up. A curious look passed behind her eyes before her expression smoothed out once more.

"What a pretty name. How are things going with you two?"

"She's…incredible. I'm in love," Nathan admitted ruefully, rocking back on his heels. "She's feeling a bit down today, I think. I was hoping to cheer her up."

Lola nodded to a new display along the wall – a row of teak wood shelves with two potted palm plants bookending them.

"Take a look at this new jewelry line. From an artist a few islands over – Irma from the Laughing Mermaid sourced it for me. She claims it is magickal and carries good wishes for the wearer."

"Ah, that's where Aurora is staying," Nathan said. "I'll take a look."

He crossed the store to study the jewelry displayed artfully on the shelves. It was a mix of high-end and affordable options, with both gold and silver metals, and precious stones mixed with pearls. One necklace kept catching his eye. It had chunky gold links, making the chain a touch sturdier than the more delicate strands next to it, and three stones nestled in a hammered gold disc. The first stone looked to be emerald, the second a citrine, and the third an aquamarine. Green, gold, and blue. It was an interesting combination and reminded Nathan of both land and sea, with the citrine representing the sun rising over the two. He returned to the counter and held it up for Lola.

"This makes me think of the island. Both land and sea, with the sun...is that citrine?"

"It is," Lola agreed, shooting him another inscrutable look. "This is a wonderful choice, but it is quite pricey. I'm not sure where you are in the relationship yet, but just so you know."

"It's fine. She's worth it," Nathan said. He wasn't lying either. He'd do anything for Aurora.

On the drive home, Nathan worried over what could be bothering Aurora. She'd come home from her swim the night before and they'd made love with an intensity that had rendered him speechless. Never before had a woman so consumed him, and his love for her was dizzying. This morning, once again, she'd reached for him – kissing him to the point of desperation. He certainly didn't mind the attention, but now he wondered what had happened during her swim. Perhaps he'd be able to get her to talk about it over lunch.

"Aurora?" Nathan called, as he kicked the door closed behind him. "I'm home."

"I'm out here," Aurora called from the deck. Nathan made his way out to the deck to find Aurora standing at the railing, staring out to the sea. He put his packages down on the lounger and crossed to her, pulling her into his arms. Nathan rested his chin on her head, enjoying her curves under his hands, and settled his palms on her stomach. A quick hitch of her breath indicated that something was amiss.

"Are you okay, Aurora?"

"I...I don't know," Aurora said, her words just a whisper. Her response worried Nathan.

"Do you want to talk about it?" Nathan pressed. *Please, talk to me, Aurora.*

"I don't know," Aurora admitted. "My thoughts are... like two eels battling each other underwater. Knots."

"Why don't we eat? I won't push you and maybe your thoughts can become untied while you relax a bit?" Nathan suggested. He pulled her over to the double lounger in the shade and Aurora lay on the cushion. She wore an emerald sarong with pink parrots scattered across the cloth, and Nathan now knew there was nothing beneath it. Aurora enjoyed being naked, and it was a constant battle to stay focused at work when she flitted by his office either in the nude or wearing a scant piece of fabric that barely covered her luscious body.

Nathan unpacked the food and returned to the kitchen for a tray, utensils, and two glasses of orange juice. He considered mimosas, but since she was already bothered by something he figured that adding alcohol to the mix probably wasn't a good idea. He found her nibbling on a strawberry, staring into the distance. Nathan tried not to be distracted by the way her lush lips surrounded the strawberry, and instead set the glasses down on the tray and spread the food out. After he'd settled next to Aurora, he turned and held up the box that Lola had wrapped a sparkly pink ribbon around.

"What's this?" Aurora asked. She shifted closer, her

shoulder brushing his, and Nathan caught her sweet scent on the wind.

"A gift. For you."

"You don't have to bring me gifts. I haven't been able to buy you anything…" Aurora pursed her lips.

"You don't have money yet to buy me gifts. But not all gifts are something you buy, Aurora. Gifts can be creating special moments or making art…it's not just about the exchange of money for a present. I just happened to see this and think of you."

"Well, I owe you a gift then," Aurora decided, pulling at the ribbon.

"No, that's not it either." Nathan laughed, poking her side so that she glanced up at him. "Gifts aren't meant to be given with an expectation of getting something back. You just do it because you love someone. That's all."

Aurora unwrapped the package and pulled the necklace out so that the gemstones caught the sunlight. Her mouth dropped open and her eyes darted to his.

"Nathan." Aurora's voice caught.

"I thought it, well…it's like you and me. See? The green for the island. Blue for the water." Nathan pointed to the pendant.

"And…the gold stone?" Aurora's voice was barely a whisper, her hand going to her stomach.

"It's the sun, I thought. It rises over both of our worlds." Dread slipped through Nathan as tears welled in Aurora's eyes. "I'm sorry. You don't like it."

"No," Aurora gasped, slipping the necklace over her neck so the pendant nestled at her exquisite cleavage. "I *love* it."

"Oh, right. Sure. Then why...why are you crying? Aurora, will you tell me what's wrong?" Nathan moved to slide an arm around her shoulder, but she pulled away, indicating she didn't want to be touched. He dropped his hands to his lap, uncertain how to proceed.

"I don't know how to say this. I don't know what to do, not really, but I feel like I have to make a decision that isn't just about me anymore," Aurora began.

"Okay?" Nathan handed her a napkin and she dabbed at the tears that now streamed across her cheeks. Her tears were such a contrast to the beautiful day that it was jarring for him. Sunlight dappled the deck, the palm leaves shifted merrily in the ocean breeze, and waves crashed at the beach. It should have been a lovely lazy morning with the woman he loved. But, as dread spread its cold fingers around his heart, he waited for what he thought might be coming. *Of course* it was coming. Aurora had always been too good to be true, hadn't she?

"I have to go home."

The words were the death knell to their relationship that he had feared, and his heart shattered.

"But...can't we figure this out? You seemed so optimistic about us..." Nathan trailed off as Aurora shook her head vehemently, her hair tumbling around her shoulders. Sweat pricked on his brow, as he tried to make sense of what was happening.

"Things have changed," Aurora said.

"What things?" Now, anger began to make its way through Nathan. Frustration at being kept in the dark, anger at her making the decision for their relationship without even speaking to him about it, and insecurity over feeling like he'd been played for a fool. They all mixed within him, one big cocktail of fury, and he tried to tamp it down so he could listen to her words.

"Nathan, I just...my people need me. I've been irresponsible to my family and my people by leaving in such a manner. It is my duty to become ruler one day, and they need me."

"That's...but...you said we could figure it out! That your family could get someone else to rule. You told me that this would be something we can manage together. That anything was possible..." Nathan sputtered, furious with Aurora for being misled.

"Maybe some things just can't be overcome," Aurora said, her turquoise eyes watery.

"That's bullshit! You never even tried. You don't even know what will happen. You barely gave this, *us*, a chance." Nathan hopped up, too angry to sit, and paced in front of the lounge chair. "And now you deliver this news like you're the only one who has a say? What about me? What about my feelings for you? I love you, Aurora. You. I want you in my life, forever. That's the truth of it. I knew in an instant that you were meant for me. It didn't take any longer than that. My heart recognized yours. It was like a part of me that had been missing all these years just showed up and completed me. And now you want to take it away? I can't..." Nathan wanted to punch something, someone, but instead he just ran his hand through his hair and tugged it hard enough to make him wince.

Aurora was openly sobbing now, and he wanted to go to her, to wipe her tears away and tell her that everything was going to be okay – but he couldn't. She was making this decision…unless…his eyes narrowed.

"There's another man, isn't there? Are you promised to someone back home? Some Mer prince that I have to kill?"

Aurora's eyes widened at his words.

"No, no, Nathan. No, I promise you…it's not that. There's nobody else."

"Then what changed? *Tell* me," Nathan demanded, poking his finger in the air to accentuate his words. "Tell me what happened between yesterday and today that sent you down this path."

"I…" Aurora's eyes were huge in her face and her lower lip trembled. "I promise you there is no other man."

"How can I trust you if you don't tell me what is really going on?" Nathan demanded.

"Trust…" Aurora whispered. She nodded once to herself and then drew her shoulders back as though to gather strength. "Nathan, I'm pregnant."

It had been the last thing he'd been expecting her to say, so he stood there in shock, his mouth hanging open like a guppy. When the moment drew out, she just watched him carefully, waiting for his reaction.

"Excuse me?" Nathan said, feeling faint.

"I'm pregnant. I'm with child. Your child. Well, *our* baby. It's why the pendant made me cry, you see. I thought the gold stone to mean our baby." Aurora fingered the pendant at her chest.

"How…" Nathan's brain tried to process, but he was being hit with so many emotions at once he didn't even know what to think. Elation, anger, fear…it was like the first time he'd ridden in the front seat on a roller coaster, and they tipped over the edge of the huge drop.

"Well, the normal way I suppose. We can get pregnant if we have sex," Aurora smiled softly at him.

"I mean…how do you know? It is so soon," Nathan said and then ran his hands through his hair once more. He was bungling this. Crossing to Aurora, he dropped to his knees in front of her and put his hands on her legs. She allowed his touch, which was a step in the right direction. "Aurora, this is not bad news. You don't have to go home. We both want children, we said we wanted children, this is a blessing for us. You don't need to leave me because of the baby. Or…do you? Is it a medical thing? Do the babies need to be birthed in the water? I'm so out of my element here. Please help me to understand," Nathan pleaded with her.

"It isn't easy for us to conceive. I need to be at home and to give birth there," Aurora explained.

"But…okay, so you give birth there. But can't you come back, after? With the baby? So I can help? I mean, it's my baby, too. Won't I get to see it? To help you? You don't have to do this alone, Aurora."

"I'm never alone, Nathan," Aurora raised her eyes to him, sadness etched on her impossibly beautiful face. "I'll always have my people. And they need me. My family will need me. This baby will need to be raised with its people and I've been told…"

"Told what? What about my people? The baby should know about me, too," Nathan found himself arguing with her.

"I've been told, by the Oracle herself, that I am the

changemaker for my people. Which means, I have no choice, Nathan. I can fight destiny all I want, but my people will need me to usher them into a new age. I must go. If I go now, it will hurt less, don't you see?" Aurora began to sob, and despite his fury with her, Nathan pulled her into his arms while she trembled against his shoulder.

"There has to be another way, Aurora. You can't just... it's not black and white. Why are you making it so?"

"I don't see how, Nathan. It's just...you *can't* even swim." The last came out as an accusation and Nathan drew back, resentment filling him at her words.

"And you didn't think I'd be willing to learn? For you? That you could help me? That as a couple we could work together and achieve our dreams? That's it then? You just unilaterally make a decision for us, and I'm supposed to fall in line? Well, that's just...it's shit, Aurora. It's unfair and not what a good partner does. I'm too mad to even look at you right now," Nathan stood and stormed inside before he said anything else that might irrevocably damage their relationship.

A baby.

His thoughts whirled in his head about what a little Mer-baby would look like, how they could raise it, what they could name it. Except, there was no *they*. Aurora had decided for them, without taking any of his feelings into account.

When he'd finally calmed down enough to return outside, he pulled up short.

Aurora was gone, the parrot sarong left dangling over the deck railing, fluttering in the breeze.

Nathan closed his eyes and wept.

CHAPTER 17

*S*he cried the whole way home.

Aurora didn't know if she was making the right choice, but she did know that she couldn't stay with Nathan. Not with this huge of a secret to reveal. Her family may forgive her some transgressions but hiding a pregnancy would destroy their bonds. And she'd realized something else. While Aurora hungered for a different life, that didn't mean she wanted to turn her back on her family. She loved them, even if they were difficult at times, and now she understood the difference in wanting more versus wanting out. For her, wanting more hadn't meant abandoning her family even if she chafed against the responsibility staying in the village would bring.

But now? She had something more to consider. Her baby. No longer were her needs and wants her own. And that is why Aurora hurried back home.

She hated how Nathan had looked at her. As though she was betraying him, breaking his heart…she could only imagine how he'd felt when he'd found her gone. She hoped he could understand how torn she was, how much she loved him, but there was no way. There was just no way to make this work. The reality was that they were of two different worlds, and her baby would need to spend time with its people.

Why can't she have both?

The stubborn voice inside her head forced her tears to fall faster. Jolie and Mirra were able to have both – why couldn't she? They weren't royals, Aurora reminded herself. Though Jolie had told her that her grandfather had been a ruler – but the structure of their tribe had been different than Aurora's. There appeared to be less weight on the blood of the ruling family, and more on the decision of the ruling group as a whole. Or at the very least, it had shifted in recent years Jolie had explained. Now, Aurora wondered if her parents would ever allow something of that nature or if they were too rooted in following the way things had always been done.

That was the problem with doing things the same way for years – eventually, change would be forced upon them. It was the difference between being proactive and reactive. Aurora feared that she was going to be the force of change, and it wouldn't likely go over well.

Aurora arrived at her village, swimming past the surprised guards, and ignoring everyone who waved to her from their various caves. Set deep in the ocean outside Triste Islands, Aurora's village was built in a tunnel of caves and swim-throughs that connected in a spider-web pattern leading to a great cavern in the middle. The main cavern was the meeting place for social events, political discussions, and basically anything that warranted bringing the Mer together. Aurora avoided that, instead taking a private corridor to her own set of rooms in the royal area. She'd barely passed through the arched doorway when her mother found her.

"Aurora! I could feel you coming..." Queen Madeline, her hair braided back from her forehead and a simple gold circlet on her crown, swam forward and embraced Aurora. "I've missed you. You bring a certain energy to our home that I do delight in. Are you well?"

"I..." Aurora brought her eyes to her mother's, tears filling them once more, and the queen understood immediately. Taking her arm, she ushered Aurora into her private chambers, ordering the guard positioned outside to ensure their privacy. Once inside, the queen nudged Aurora into a hammock swing woven of kelp and seaweed and curled up next to her.

Aurora leaned into her mother's arms, enjoying the gentle sway of the hammock in the water for a bit, and tried to gather her thoughts.

"Won't you tell me what's made you cry?"

"I've met someone." Aurora figured it was best to start there, before surprising her with the news of the baby.

"Ah, of course. Love. It's bound to bring tears at some point, or you're not doing it right," Queen Madeline mused.

Aurora tilted her head to look at her mother in surprise. It wasn't the response she had expected.

"You're not mad at me for falling in love with a human?"

"It's a surprise, I'll admit." The queen paused and thought about it. "But no, I'm not mad. Disconcerted, perhaps. I had hoped you'd find your person with the Mer, but you tried, didn't you?"

"I did. Nothing clicked."

"I want to see you happy, Aurora. I think that finding the right partner matters. They are so intricately entwined with everything that you do, well, you should never settle. Love matters. If this man you've found on land is the one, well, I'm not sure what that will look like yet, but I bet we can make it work."

"Do you really think so?" Hope bloomed in Aurora's chest.

"I don't know. That's not me being difficult, that's just me being honest with you, Aurora. I don't know how your father will take it. I don't know what that will mean for you as a ruler in the future. It might not be possible for you to rule with your time divided between land and sea. Or maybe you bring on trusted advisors to rule during your absences."

"Or maybe I don't rule at all?" Aurora asked. Her mother's lips pressed into a thin line.

"That's not my preference, Aurora. I've always seen you as the next in line to rule over our people. You've been brought up for this role."

"I understand that, but if I didn't want it?" Aurora pushed.

"I...I don't know. It upsets me." The queen crossed her arms over her chest and looked down. "I won't lie to you about my feelings, Aurora. It will upset me greatly if you choose not to rule."

"I figured as much," Aurora's heart sank.

"But, this isn't about me," the queen admitted. "This is

about you. And if I put my queenly duties aside and simply speak to you as a mother? Well, then, I want what is best for you. I can't be the one to determine that. Only you can. And, as someone who is meant to be queen, well, you'll need to get comfortable with making difficult choices. It might not be easy to stand up to your father and me. But if this is what you want, well, you'll need to fight for it."

"You're telling me to push back?" Aurora arched a brow at Queen Madeline.

"You're a grown woman, Aurora. As a leader, you'll need to start with yourself first. Now, tell me about this man."

"His name is Nathan. He's very handsome – large and muscular – hugging him feels like home," Aurora sighed, smiling as she thought about him. "He listens to me, encourages me to question things, and helps me to learn. He…he cares about me. Deeply. I think I broke his heart."

"You were careless with his love? That's unkind, Aurora." Queen Madeline made a sound of disgust.

"I…I think I was. I've been very distraught in thinking about how I can live in both worlds, and then, well… everything changed."

"I hope what changed was important enough to hurt this man. He sounds like an excellent candidate for you, Aurora. Particularly if he is patient with your insatiable curiosity."

"Oh, he is. And…" Aurora turned and clasped her mother's hands. "I'm pregnant."

Joy flooded Queen Madeline's face, and she pulled Aurora close, crying into her hair.

"Aurora! That's incredible news. I can't believe it! Oh,

of course you came home. I understand now. It makes so much more sense. You're with child! What miraculous news this is. Oh, my darling, you're going to be a mother. We'll very much welcome this baby, as I'm sure you know. We've had so few births here in recent years."

"I know…" Aurora, for the first time, allowed herself to feel joy about her pregnancy. She'd known her mother would be happy at some point but was pleased to hear support offered so quickly. "I just…it's Nathan's baby, too. And I came here because everything feels unsettled and torn apart, yet now I've left him behind. He can't reach me, can't speak to me…he can't even swim, Mother."

"Say it isn't so? A man who cannot swim. What is the point of living by the water if you can't go into it?" Queen Madeline wondered.

"You can understand my dilemma then. How is he going to be a father to this child? If he can't even get in the water?"

"Yet, in the same breath, he can father the child on land, can he not? That will be a part of the baby, too," Queen Madeline pointed out.

"I know…I *know*…I just…" Aurora shrugged a shoulder. She bit her lip and tried to calm herself, but her emotions raced all over the place. "I needed to come back here and speak to you. To Father. To understand how to move forward."

"Does Nathan think you're going back to him?" Queen Madeline asked.

"No," Aurora said, her voice cracking. The tears came once more, and the queen rocked Aurora like a child.

"You'll fix it. Or maybe that's for the better. I don't yet

know. I've got to spend some time with my thoughts as well. It's quite a conundrum you've brought us, isn't it?"

"Yes," Aurora said. "I'm sorry."

"Don't be. Life does tend to get a bit mundane down here, doesn't it? This will liven things up nicely."

When Aurora pulled back, looking askance at her mother, Queen Madeline chuckled.

"You aren't the only one prone to fits of boredom, darling. We all just handle it differently. Now, tell me everything about your time on land and we'll figure out how to approach your father. I'll let you in on a little secret – he's softer-hearted than you realize."

"Is he? He always seems so commanding," Aurora murmured.

"Of course he does. That's his job. But don't you worry, Aurora. I have my ways to sway him. Once you decide just what it is you want, we'll figure out our approach with your father. But I suggest you don't wait long, you'll be showing soon enough. A baby!" the queen marveled. "What joy you have brought to our village."

Aurora bit her lip as the queen prattled on about babies. Nathan tugged at her thoughts. Already she missed him – would he – *could* he – ever understand her decision?

CHAPTER 18

"*I* need you to teach me."

"Nathan!" Jolie exclaimed, looking up from her laptop as Nathan exploded into the kitchen door unannounced. "Teach you what? What's going on?"

"She didn't tell you?" Nathan's breath heaved in his chest. He'd run up the beach once he'd seen Aurora was gone, hoping to find the answers he sought at the Laughing Mermaid.

"Tell us what?" Mirra asked from where she stood by the kitchen sink. He hadn't even seen her there.

"Aurora left. She's gone home."

"Oh, Nathan." Mirra's face fell, and she crossed the room to give him a hug. Nathan accepted it, sweaty though he was, and wished it was Aurora he was holding in his arms.

"Sit," Jolie ordered while Mirra left his side to pick up a tea pot. Soon, the women had a cup of tea, a plate of cookies, and sympathetic looks for him.

"She didn't come here," Nathan stated again.

"No, we didn't see her at all. She must have just gone into the water. Rude, really, when you think about it. We've been quite helpful to her," Jolie said, tapping a finger on the table.

"Yeah, well, I also thought it was rude when she dropped the bomb that she was pregnant and in the next instant, she's disappeared." Nathan dropped his chin to his hands.

"What!" Mirra clapped her hands, and even Jolie beamed at him, pounding him raucously on the back.

"Congrats, Daddy," Jolie said.

"Not quite. She doesn't think I'm suited to fathering this child. She left me to go home. Says I can't even swim, so how can we have a life together?" Nathan bit off a corner of a cookie morosely.

"Well, that's not really fair, is it? I mean the baby needs to be on land, too, right? And you can learn to swim, can't you? Is that an option for you?" Mirra asked, a furrow in her brow.

"Yes, that's what I'd like for you to teach me. Can you teach me to swim? I need help – and like not swim teacher once a week help. I need to learn to swim, and I have to figure out a way to go after her. She doesn't just get to decide what's best for our relationship and our baby without my input. Granted, I was stunned when she told me, but she barely gave me any time to process before she took off." Nathan rubbed a hand over his face. He just wanted Aurora to come back, he wanted to hold her, he wanted to promise her that everything would work out.

"I'm assuming she panicked. I don't see Aurora as being a deliberately mean person," Mirra said.

"But what she did is mean," Jolie argued. "That's not fair to him at all. To just take off? After news like that? It's not great, Mirra."

"No, it's not great. But I imagine she's scared. Emotions are probably running high with the pregnancy, too. Plus, you have to remember she's meant to rule her people. Her parents only gave her two weeks here."

"They what?" Nathan lifted his head.

"Her parents..." Mirra trailed off after realizing that Nathan hadn't been privy to this information. "We, uh, confronted them one night. They'd been calling for her on the water..."

"The sound that night?" Nathan interrupted, thinking back to their walk home from the bar and when Aurora had stopped in her tracks. "The mother calling for her baby?"

"Yes, they called for her. She went to them, with us by her side, and we negotiated for more time for her here. She needed to spend more time with you, and to learn what she wanted to do with her life. Her parents granted her two weeks," Jolie explained.

"So that's all we really had anyway? Two weeks? And she knew this and didn't tell me?"

"Well, that's kind of on me," Jolie admitted, smiling weakly at Nathan. "I told her that once her father saw how happy she was on land, he wouldn't be able to say no to her staying longer. She likely didn't want to worry you with it all."

"It would have been nice to know," Nathan mumbled.

"Nathan...what do you want right now?" Mirra asked. "How can we help you?"

"I…" Nathan looked at the two women before him. "I want to go after her. I want to fight for her. I agree that I don't think that Aurora is purposely doing these things with malice intended. I'm hurting. *This* hurts. But I also can't know how she is feeling or what she is thinking if I don't go to her. She needs to know that love means standing for each other even when the other hurts us. Or swimming for each other, in this instance."

"It's true, isn't it? Sometimes you do hurt the ones you love. I don't think this is intentional, Nathan. I think our girl is hurting as much as you are," Mirra agreed.

"I need to show her she doesn't have to do this alone," Nathan insisted.

Mirra and Jolie looked at each other.

"Well?" Jolie asked, raising an eyebrow at her sister.

"I'll take morning lessons – you take evening?" Mirra asked.

"Perfect," Jolie said. Turning, she patted Nathan's arm. "You just got yourself two swim coaches. What's next?"

"I have a plan…I think." Nathan began to outline the idea that had taken shape in his mind.

THE DAYS SLIPPED INTO WEEKS. Nathan took extended time off from work and focused only on learning one thing – how to swim. His body slimmed down, and he ate voraciously for he was constantly training. Initially, the training had been nothing more than Mirra or Jolie pulling him off the floor of his pool as he floundered, choking on water, until slowly he'd gotten over his fear of putting his head underwater.

He didn't have a reason to be scared of swimming, not really. It was more that it had built up into something so huge in his mind because his whole life he'd been unable to do this one thing. Which meant he'd shied away from water, or water activities, and that on its own, had managed to feed his fear.

"And yet you rented a villa with a pool," Jolie pointed out when he surfaced. It had been over three weeks of incessant training, and finally, Nathan had been able to hold his breath underwater for a minute. The sisters had decided on two different types of training. The first was to overcome fear, the second was the mechanisms of the basic swim strokes. When they felt he was ready, they were going to take him into the ocean and practice there, because, as they pointed out – his pool had pristine conditions. There were no waves, or sea life, or currents to panic him. But if he was going to try and spend some time in the ocean – the number one thing he needed to work on was his panic response. Luckily, once Nathan felt comfortable holding his breath underwater, the rest had come more naturally to him. An avid learner, he'd spent time researching, watching podcasts and reading books about swimming, and now he spent his nights actively visualizing swimming out into the ocean.

And missing Aurora.

The longer they were apart, the more he worried she'd move on from him. That forgetting him would make her and their baby's life easier. Maybe everything he was doing right now was for nothing. But Nathan had to at least try.

"Maybe I somehow knew I needed to have the pool?" Nathan shrugged, wiping the water from his face.

"You're ready," Jolie declared. She'd hopped up on the side of the pool and swung her legs in the water nonchalantly.

"Wait...what? Really?" Nathan froze.

"Yes, tonight we start. You need to learn how to be in the ocean. At night."

"Shouldn't we start during the day?" Nathan protested.

"Nope. Night is the time when the mermaids swim closer to land. The day will always be easier. But we are not working you up to a night swim, we're starting with that."

"Baptism by fire," Nathan muttered.

"Pretty much. See you tonight. Our place," Jolie trilled as she sauntered away, leaving Nathan with a stomach full of nerves. He pulled himself from the pool and toweled off, before sitting at his laptop at the table under the umbrella. If the sisters thought he was ready for the ocean swim, then it was time for the second part of his plan. Nathan pulled up the website he'd found with the real estate listings for Triste Island. His choices were scant, but Nathan didn't care so long as he had internet for work. Picking up his phone, he called the number on the website.

LATER THAT DAY, Nathan stood, heart hammering, on the sandy beach. He looked down at a wave that rolled in, almost touching his toes, before retreating across the sand. He took several deep breaths, calming himself. Aurora was out there. This was her home, and if he loved her, then he needed to do this. He *would* do this.

Mirra and Jolie waited for him in the water, allowing him to enter in his own time. He appreciated their restraint. He'd had coaches in the past who were so pushy they'd turned him away from a sport. Everyone learned at a different pace, and he was grateful for the sisters and their dedication to helping him become a swimmer. Now, as the moon shone brightly over the ocean, he followed the path of light that sparkled across the surface. First one step, and then another, the water swishing around his ankles.

Fed up with himself, Nathan lunged forward, running until the water hit his hips, and then he dove beneath the surface. At the last moment he remembered to shut his mouth and eyes, and he floated for a moment, disoriented, before he bobbed to the surface next to Mirra and Jolie.

"Well, that was unexpected," Jolie laughed.

"I was sick of taking it slow," Nathan explained.

"You certainly made a splash," Mirra said.

"You won't get points for a great entrance though. A bit rough around the edges," Jolie said.

"Extra points for enthusiasm though," Mirra demurred.

It was then that Nathan realized they were keeping him talking so that he didn't think about the fact that he was treading water in the dark ocean. The moment he did, he slipped beneath the surface, but using what he'd learned, he kicked back to the top.

"You were distracting me, weren't you?" Nathan asked. He forced himself to work on the steady pattern of treading water as he'd been taught. Experimenting, Nathan rolled onto his back and realized it was also easy to float that way so long as he moved his arms and legs gently and breathed.

"Figured you were doing such a good job that it would be best not to draw attention to it," Jolie said from his side. Just her head showed above the water, and he wondered if she was in mermaid form or not.

"I feel more…floaty," Nathan said.

"Saltwater makes you more buoyant," Mirra explained. "Are you ready for your swim?"

And Nathan realized with a start that he was – he was ready for his swim in the dark ocean at night with two mermaids. A twist he'd never imagined coming in his life. This was one step closer to showing Aurora just how much he loved her, so, yeah, he was more than ready.

It was time to go get his woman.

CHAPTER 19

A gull cried above him, swooping slowly over where Nathan stood, his hands gripping the railing. He stared out to sea wondering just how close he was to Aurora's village.

The last three days had been chaotic at best. His stomach still twisted in knots over the six-seater flight he'd taken from Siren Island to Triste Island. The pilot had told him to expect it to be quiet after he'd dropped him off, but Nathan had no idea just how small he'd been talking. With fewer than one thousand full-time residents, Triste Island was nearly deserted though it did have a few paved roads, one supermarket, and three restaurants. Most of the homes were clustered around the small square at the downtown harbor, but Nathan had chosen a home further down the beach that would afford him some privacy.

Privacy from what, he wondered, as he hadn't seen another person since he'd moved here except when he'd gone to the supermarket for food. The real estate agent had already arranged for the internet to be hooked up when he arrived, so Nathan hadn't needed much else.

The three-bedroom villa was surprisingly modern for how back in time Triste felt. With whitewashed stone walls, rough-hewn exposed wood beams in the ceiling, and large windows that opened to the breeze – the space suited him. It would be good for Aurora, too, because the garden was lined with thick oleander bushes and palm trees that ran almost to the sea, blocking the view of anyone further down the beach. Which meant when Aurora would come to land, she'd have a protected entrance. It had been the garden that had sold Nathan on the property, and he'd paid for it with cash.

Not rented.

Bought.

He didn't care if that made him stupid, or impulsive, or any of the other things he was sure his friends would call him if he'd told them about this. The one thing he was certain of was that Aurora needed to know that he would show up for her. Even if she hurt him. Even if she pushed him away. And if she still said no, at the very least, he would demand the right to see their baby. She couldn't deny him that, at least he hoped not, and that had cemented his decision to buy a house on Triste. For better or worse, his family lived here now.

The sea had been rough the last few days. Each night, when Nathan had worked up the courage to walk to the edge of the water, he'd watched – as the sisters had instructed him – the pattern of the waves and the direction of the water. They'd taught him about undertow, and currents, and all the things he needed to be aware of when it came time to enter the ocean.

Today the winds had abated, and the sea was as smooth as glass. It was almost too calm, Nathan thought, but perhaps that was just nerves making him question every detail. It was also a month to the day since Aurora had left him. It still hurt, knowing she didn't trust him enough to work on things together, but maybe he needed to earn her trust. From everything he'd gathered, humans hadn't been particularly friendly to the Mer through the years. Maybe that added another layer to her anxiety when she'd discovered she was pregnant. Either way, tonight was his night. He was going to swim into the sea and call for Aurora. Just like her parents had done when she'd gone missing. And if she didn't come, that was fine. He was going to go out there every night until she did.

He really hoped she'd come tonight. Swimming still wasn't his favorite thing, though he was proud of the strides he'd made. As the sun kissed the horizon, Nathan took a few calming breaths before picking up the life jacket that both Mirra and Jolie had insisted he wear in the water when they weren't around to supervise him. Not that he'd put up much of a fight – he also felt safer with the jacket on even if it made his movements a touch clunkier.

He'd thought Siren Island was quiet. But this? It was an entirely different type of quiet – almost eerily so. Nathan stood where the water met the beach, his feet sinking ever so slightly into the damp sand and absorbed his surroundings. There were no car horns, random laughter, or strains of music carried to him across the water.

Occasionally, the call of a gull would break the silence, but otherwise, the ocean was dead calm – and he was alone.

Very much alone.

The last bit made him swallow hard, however he remembered his training. Swim against any current, flip on his back if he became overwhelmed, and take it slow. There was no need to burn himself out in a rush to find Aurora. Jolie had suggested he swim far enough out that he was in deep water, but not so far as to not be able to return to land as needed. Both sisters had insisted on a phone call at his return each night, no matter the time. They worried for him – and he couldn't blame them. This might be the riskiest thing he'd ever done in his life.

Nathan shook his head, pushing those thoughts aside, and worked on visualizing his swim and how to keep calm if his nerves kicked up. Slowly, he stepped forward into the water, until he was standing in waist-deep water. The ocean was a touch cooler here, but it rejuvenated him, forcing him to stay focused on the mission at hand. He ducked his head under the surface, getting his face and hair wet, and he bobbed gently in the water. The jacket certainly did its job, but he quickly found that it was a touch easier to swim if he rotated on his back and kicked backwards. Slow and steady, Nathan reminded himself, kicking further away from shore as the last shreds of sunlight danced across the turquoise water. A breeze kicked up, swooping over the hills of Triste, and rippling the ocean's surface. It was cold, much colder than the norm, and unease prickled at Nathan's neck.

It took longer than Nathan had expected, but eventually he found himself in dark water, far from shore. At once, the foolishness of his actions gripped him, and he wondered if he'd well and truly lost his mind. What was he, a man who only just recently learned to swim, doing in the middle of the ocean – at night – on an island where nobody was looking out for him? Panic threatened, its ugly tendrils curling around his heart, and he closed his eyes to focus solely on his breathing for a moment. The wind buffeted across the water, blowing harder now, an eerie moan accompanying it.

Once Nathan finally centered himself again, he opened his eyes. To his horror, he saw where the eerie sound had come from. Rolling black clouds, illuminated from within by sharp spikes of lightning, raced across the sea, blocking out the stars.

A squall.

He'd forgotten to check the weather radar before he'd entered the ocean. This explained why the water had been so unnaturally calm – the storm had sucked all the wind to it. Now, it barreled towards him like a herd of bison racing across the plains, and Nathan knew real fear.

"Aurora!" Nathan bellowed, his cry carrying across the water. He screamed again, her name coming from the depths of his soul, as the storm neared. Over and over he cried, hoping beyond hope that she could reach him before the storm hit. But then…he stopped – a thought occurring to him.

Why would he bring her to the surface during a storm when she carried their child? What kind of man was he that he would put them in danger like that? Gulping as the water roiled, salty water spraying him in the face, Nathan turned to shore and began to swim, desperate to return to land. Another wave slapped him in the face, and Nathan gulped seawater on his next breath, choking as the salty brine burned his throat. His eyes stung, and he couldn't see well without his glasses as it was, but the wall of rain that hit him with the force of a Mack truck sealed the deal. Nathan was well and truly lost at sea, blind to land, and barely able to gasp for air as the storm surrounded him. The ocean tossed him about, like a wayward sock in a washing machine, and all Nathan could do was hold his life jacket and try to stop from inhaling salt water. Panic gripped him, and he closed his eyes against the next big wave that towered over his head. When it hit, the force of the wave flipped Nathan over, tumbling him right into the next wave, and soon he barely knew up from down. Lights danced before his eyes as he tried to catch a breath, but the ocean was too much for him.

Darkness claimed him.

athan.

Aurora's head went up, hearing his call reverberate through the ocean, and she was out of her room and barreling through the corridor to the front gates without a second thought.

Nathan was here and he was calling for her.

Aurora's shoulders tensed as she approached the guards.

"Princess…" The guards bowed their heads at her.

"I'm needed. I must leave here." Aurora waited to see if they would try to stop her – if her father had ordered her to be kept here under guard. When one guard swam forward, her stomach twisted. She didn't want to have to make a scene, but she would do so if necessary.

"I'm under orders to go with you should you wish to leave." The guard bowed his head once more.

"You're not to interfere with whatever I choose to do?" Aurora questioned. This was new.

"No, princess. I'm here for your safety, and that of the

child you carry. My instructions are to protect, but not to detain."

For her father, that was a compromise, and one that Aurora would accept. She couldn't make rash decisions now that she was with child, and it was hard to say what she would encounter when she reached the surface. Motioning for the guard to follow, Aurora swam toward where Nathan called to her.

When the sound abruptly cut off, worry gripped her. Was Nathan on a boat or in the water? Aurora opened her senses to the ocean, and that's when she realized what was happening.

Nathan had come for her.

And a storm raged at the surface.

The implications of those two events slammed into her, and Aurora increased her speed, trying to narrow in on where she'd heard his call. Her tracking ability was excellent, but still, when she surfaced to bedlam, it was impossible to see if Nathan was caught in the churning water.

"Princess." The guard grabbed her arm when she went to surface once more. "You must be careful. There's lightning striking the water. You can't go to the surface right now."

The two Mer hovered at a depth well below where the storm gathered the water to its breast, tossing it back down in catastrophic waves, and looked at each other.

"Guard. The father of my baby is caught in this storm. He's human and could be in mortal danger. We must help him."

"At your own peril?" the guard asked. At least he was

communicating with her instead of dragging her back to the village.

"Yes, at my own peril." Aurora held his eyes, lifting her chin in challenge.

"Are you ordering me to assist you?" The guard phrased his words carefully, and Aurora now understood he wanted to help but not risk her father's wrath.

"This is an order," Aurora said, and the guard gave her a sharp nod in assent. "We need to find him, and if he is in danger, we're bringing him home with us."

"How?" Confusion crossed the guards face.

"My friends on Siren Island taught me. It's old magick, but it's how the Mer once interacted with the humans." Aurora spoke as she swam, scanning the turbulent waters above her. "I'll breathe it into his lungs, giving him the ability to survive underwater, and once in the village, we'll take him to the sanctuary for reprieves and to refresh the magick."

The Sanctuary was the only cave in the village that had one tunnel that ran directly from the surface, connecting it with a cavern on land. Because of how it was protected, air filtered freely into the room from land, while strong magick – the Oracle's magick – kept the entrance sealed from water rushing in from their village. Aurora had always wondered why there was a need for such a room, but now it made perfect sense. Which also made her question just how many times the Mer had actually brought humans to the village. It seemed there might be more to their history than Aurora had been taught.

Shoving those questions aside for another day, Aurora stopped when she caught a flash of fluorescent orange being tossed about in the surface. Her heart skipped, and she pointed, racing upward. The guard followed, matching her speed, and when Aurora saw a limp body in the water she cried out.

"Nathan!" Aurora shouted as she broke the surface straight into pandemonium. Waves higher than a house crashed, one after another, with barely any time between them. The sea rolled, as though someone was pulling a carpet out from beneath them, and Aurora almost lost sight of Nathan. Quickly, she swam to his side and hooked an arm through his. The guard surfaced next to her, and immediately caught Nathan's other arm, holding his body tightly.

"Nathan," Aurora gasped, searching for a response. His eyes remained closed, his face a stark white against the dark water. Another wave crashed over them, and Aurora realized he was drowning. There was no time to waste.

"Get this off him!" Aurora screamed, knowing the orange vest he wore was meant to keep people on the surface. No way would she be able to get him to her village if she had to battle a flotation device. Her hand scrambled at the buckles, shaking, and she held tight as another wave tossed them about like a child throwing her toys out of the pram. They rolled in the water, the guard holding tightly to the three of them, and surfaced once more.

"Princess, let me." The guard brandished a sharpened abalone shell, set in a carved gold handle, and neatly sliced through the straps of the life jacket. It was a magickal dagger, one meant to cut through anything in its path, and had been designed after one too many Mer had been lost to dangerous trawling nets. She'd been foolish to leave the village without hers.

As soon as the life jacket broke free, Nathan began to sink.

Aurora caught him, sinking with him, her lips on his. Holding his face in her hands, she teased his mouth open, and breathed her magick into his lungs.

Goddess of the Moon, Mother of the Sea, I invoke your powers, to let this man breathe.

Aurora continued to breathe into Nathan, taking the water from his lungs, and replacing it with her magick while the guard propelled them away from the surface and toward the village. Only when they'd crossed through the gates, her people surrounding her, did Aurora break contact.

"The Sanctuary!" Aurora shouted, spying her mother through the crowd. Understanding dawned on her mother's face, and the queen instantly took charge, clearing the way while Aurora returned her lips to Nathan's. Terrified the spell wouldn't work, she didn't want to risk not giving him air until they'd reached the safe room.

They tumbled through the barrier to the Sanctuary, the guard taking the brunt of their fall, and Aurora lay on the ground, gasping.

"Is he…?" the guard asked, nodding to Nathan.

"I don't know. Please, if the healer is near – can you get her? And thank you for your service. I'm indebted to you," Aurora said. The guard bowed his head and left, diving back into the water through the door in the floor.

"Nathan," Aurora said. She eased backward, slipping halfway through the door so she hung at the floor like on the edge of a pool, and then willed herself to transform. Once she had her legs, she pulled herself back into the Sanctuary and crossed to Nathan, cradling his head on her belly.

"Oh, Nathan. I'm so sorry I left you," Aurora whispered, planting kisses on his cheeks, her tears dripping on his face. "What a foolish foolish woman I am. I can't believe you came for me. Please, please, please...I need you to be safe. Please wake up, Nathan. Say my magick is strong enough."

A flutter at his eyelids had hope blooming in her heart, and when a ragged breath escaped his lips, Aurora sobbed.

"Princess."

The healer, a powerful Mer witch in her own right, poked her head from the water. Aurora beckoned her close.

The cavern itself didn't have much for comforts when it came to the human world, but the floor had been lined with soft sea grasses, and light shone from enchanted torches on the rocky walls. It wasn't a large room, but it was enough.

"He breathes," Aurora said, blinking back tears. "But barely."

"That's a good sign." The healer pressed both her hands to Nathan's chest and closed her eyes as though she was listening. When she opened them again, her irises glowed golden. "Your magick is strong, Aurora. You called upon the heart of the ocean and our mother moon goddess. Love strengthens this spell. I'm going to clear the rest of the water from his lungs and heal the damage. It will only take a moment."

"Is it bad? The damage?" Aurora whispered. She'd

learned very quickly what lack of air could do to a human's body when Nathan had explained to her one night why so many people feared swimming.

"No, my dear. You've reached him in time. However, as I've been given the gift to heal – there's no sense in not using it to the best of my abilities. Hush now and let me work."

Aurora gasped as Nathan's chest glowed from within, the healer's hands pressing against his skin, and she knew it was his soul she saw. Would it leave him this night? Tears ran down her face, but she continued to whisper words of love to Nathan, while also holding a hand to her womb. Reaching up, the healer turned Nathan's head, and water poured from his mouth in a sickly little stream. He wretched, and more followed, but Aurora didn't look away.

Please breathe on your own.

When he shuddered, dropping back to the floor, Aurora could have cheered. His chest rose in even compressions now, though his eyes remained closed.

"He'll rest now. Give him time." The healer eyed her curiously. "You haven't been to see me."

"Ah, no, I haven't." Aurora cupped her stomach, a fine trembling starting in her limbs now that the danger had passed.

"May I?" The healer held up her hands, nodding at Aurora's stomach that had swelled quite quickly. It wasn't uncommon for Mer to show their pregnancies early on, but even Aurora had been surprised at the growth. There had been no hiding the news from their people, and the whole village was excited about the impending birth.

"Yes, that's fine," Aurora said. She supposed it was best to check the baby as well, as this experience had been quite traumatic. She felt fine, if totally exhausted, but she wasn't hurt.

The healer's hands were cool against her skin, but her touch was gentle. Aurora could feel her magick, like a gentle probing, as she murmured to herself.

"Is everything fine? The baby is safe?" Aurora asked, when the moment drew out longer than she expected. The healer rocked back, crossing her arms over her chest and she tilted her head at Aurora. The woman was of an indeterminate age – richly beautiful – but ageless in the way of Mer when they'd already aged several decades.

"Your babies are safe," the healer clarified.

"Ba…babies?" Aurora stammered.

"Yes, my dear. I wish you'd come to me sooner or this wouldn't be the surprise that I see it is." The healer gave her a chiding look. "You should know there's special care and regimens I like my mothers to follow."

"Did you say babies? There's more than one?" Aurora said, shaking her head slowly. Surely she'd only envisioned the one glowing ball of light in her womb? Had there been another hiding behind it?

"Here. Come with me," the healer said. Placing her hand on top of Aurora's she brought it back to the womb. "Open your senses and I will show you."

Aurora closed her eyes and focused on her womb, opening herself to the magick there. Another light entered, a white one with golden threads, and this was the healer. She followed it, as the healer showed her where the glowing light she had mistaken for one, was actually two nestled tightly together. Her heart trembled as tears poured down her face once more.

Two babies.

Two worlds.

Two hearts bound together.

Aurora squeezed Nathan's hand as she opened her eyes, nodding her thanks to the healer. Overcome with emotion, she couldn't bring herself to speak.

"Send for me once he wakes."

"I'll do so," Aurora whispered. "Thank you…I can't begin to…"

"Shh, it's my gift. I'm only grateful I was able to help in this instance." With that, the healer dove through the doorway and Aurora was left cradling Nathan in her lap.

She had no idea how long she sat there, kissing his face, singing to him…anything to lure him awake from the abyss he lingered in. So many emotions knotted in her stomach…relief, anxiety, happiness…and, well, love. Just pure love. For Nathan. For their babies.

What a fool she'd been to leave him. Aurora had convinced herself that it was for the best – for the good of their baby and for Nathan. What kind of life would he have if he stayed with her? Forever chained to Triste Island, only seeing her half the time because she'd have to rule her people. It wasn't fair to him, or at least she'd thought at the time. Now, seeing how he'd risked his life to find her, she realized that she'd been the unfair one. It wasn't right of her to decide what was best for Nathan without seeking his input. He was his own man, and he could make his own decisions.

Stupid though they may be…

Aurora glared down at Nathan, suddenly furious at him for putting his life in danger, and that was the moment he chose to pop his eyes open. He blinked at her, confusion clouding his vision, and then his brow furrowed.

"Why are you looking at me like that?" Nathan croaked. He tried to move, but Aurora put her hand on his shoulder, staying him.

"Because you're an idiot, that's why," Aurora said. This pure, sweet, precious man had almost died trying to find her.

"Nice to see you as well, Aurora," Nathan grimaced.

Aurora burst into tears.

"Hey, now. Hold on. Just..." Nathan heaved himself up, shifting so he could put his arms around Aurora, and gathered her close. "Shh, shh. It's going to be just fine, Aurora. Where...where are we? What even happened? I was...oh my god, am I dead?"

"No, I saved you." Aurora sniffled into his arm.

"That was nice of you," Nathan said, pressing a kiss to her head. "But where are we?"

"We're in my village. In the Sanctuary room." Aurora pulled back in time to see Nathan visibly blanch at her words.

"We're...under..." Nathan stuttered, looking around the cavern.

"Yes, it's spring-fed, well air-fed. From the surface." Aurora gestured with her hand to the ceiling.

"But how does the water stay out?" Nathan asked, staring at the hole in the floor.

"Nathan! Is that what is most important right now?" Aurora demanded, frustrated with him.

"Well, yes, kind of. I need to understand how to not die," Nathan pointed out.

"You can start with not swimming out into the water in the middle of a storm," Aurora stood and shouted, tossing her hands in the air. "What were you thinking?"

"In all fairness, the water was dead calm when I swam out," Nathan began and then winced when Aurora glared at him.

"Nathan! You don't even know how to swim. What were you thinking? How could you put yourself in danger that way? If the sea is that calm, it usually means something's afoot. Did you even look at the weather? What are you even doing here?" Aurora rapid-fired questions at him, working herself up until her chest was heaving. Nathan leaned forward and grabbed her hand, tugging her back to him so that she could sit in his lap. "I shouldn't sit on you. You almost died."

"And I haven't had you in my arms for an entire month. Plus, since I almost died, I'd think you'd be nicer to me," Nathan said, and then brushed a tear away from her cheek as Aurora continued to cry. "To answer your questions…I made Jolie and Mirra teach me how to swim. I'm not great, but I'm stable at it. I wanted to show you that I am committed to this working and since that seemed to be a sticking point for you, I took off from work and devoted all my time to learning how to swim."

"Oh, Nathan," Aurora said, understanding dawning. He didn't care about her leaving in a fit. Instead, he'd worked hard to address one of her concerns and shown up for her. She really *was* horrible. "That had to have been so very difficult for you."

"It was, but you are worth it to me." Nathan leaned in so that his forehead touched hers. "And no, I didn't check the weather and yes, I'm an idiot for not doing so. That was the most terrifying experience of my life."

"I almost lost you," Aurora whispered.

"I'm right here. And I've been right here all along, Aurora. You only had to talk to me," Nathan said. He was so close that the color of his eyes blurred. She leaned a few inches back so he could come into focus for her – much like her new understanding of what she wanted for her life.

"Nathan." Aurora pressed one hand to his chest, over his heart, and took a shuddering breath. "I owe you a huge apology. As in, massive. I was so short-sighted in what my options were for my future and I, well, I panicked. I couldn't see how we would work together, not with the babies, and…"

Nathan grabbed her shoulders, cutting her off.

"What did you just say?"

"Oh goddess, Nathan! I just found out when the healer came for you," Aurora exclaimed, searching his eyes. "There's two. We have two babies on the way."

"Twins," Nathan breathed. Aurora waited, hoping he would be happy for them. When a smile broke his handsome face, the last bit of tension eased from her shoulders.

"Twins. But…" Aurora held up a finger when Nathan leaned in to try and kiss her. "I haven't finished my apology."

"Aurora, it's fine…" Nathan tried to brush it away.

"No, it's *not* fine." Aurora drew herself up and once more pressed a hand to his heart. "I don't yet know if I'm going to step into a leadership role for my people. Or what that will look like for me, or us, in the future. But, as a Mer, and a woman who is proud of who she is, I need to finish my apology to you. It's important that I own my actions, and not try and hide from them. What I did was wrong, Nathan. I've thought about it every day since. I've obsessed over our last conversation. I...I can't tell you how many times I've almost come to you. But I didn't. I thought you must be so mad at me. Or that you would move on and find someone else. I told myself it was for the best, really. That you would find a partner on land who could live a full life with you, not one divided between land and sea. And so I lied to myself and to you. I lied when I told myself that I would be happy for you if you found someone else to love. I lied to myself when I said that coming home was best for me and the babies. Because it's not. It hasn't been. I've been miserable and everyone can see it. My mother's worried I'm dying of a broken heart, I've been barely eating..." Aurora could barely see Nathan through the tears that welled in her eyes. He leaned forward. "No, let me finish. I think...I've been punishing myself. Because I know that I've a hurt a good man, no, the *best* man, and I don't deserve you." The tears spilled over, but still Aurora held herself back, needing to know that Nathan truly heard her words.

He seemed to understand this need and didn't push her, instead bringing his hands together to twiddle his thumbs as he listened.

"May I speak?" Nathan finally asked.

"Just one more thing...I love you. I haven't stopped loving you. But maybe I didn't understand how my love could be enough for you. For us. For all of this. I felt torn between duty and love, and I made the wrong choice." Aurora hung her head.

"Okay, that's enough self-flagellation for now." Nathan reached over and tilted her chin up with his finger so she could meet his eyes once more. "Aurora, yes, you hurt me."

Aurora winced, feeling his words slice through her. She opened her mouth to speak, but he brought his finger to her lips to quiet her.

"You hurt me," Nathan continued. "But I'd like to think that we can forgive as well. There are going to be times in the course of our relationship where we hurt each other. That's just…that's life. It's not all sunshine and rainbows and calm waters. I hated that you left me. But I understood. You'd only just been able to explore a whole new world. We fell in love so fast, and this whole time we knew that you had duties back home. You told me about your life here, and I understood the risk. That you may have to leave one day. That you might be called upon to rule. And still…" Nathan traced her lips with his finger. "And still, I loved. Because love doesn't mean having it all figured out ahead of time. Love means figuring it out together. But you have to talk to me, Aurora. You can't make decisions for our relationship and future without talking to me first."

"I see that now." Aurora's voice cracked. "I was just raised…to be a leader, I guess. To make decisions without people questioning them. And I've learned, now, that is a really dangerous path to go down. We need to question our leaders and our leaders need to be comfortable with being questioned. When I made the choice to leave you, I was doing so as a ruler. And not a good one. Because I was only really thinking about myself, and yes, what maybe my Mer people needed, but even then – I didn't really understand what they needed. If anything, there has been one benefit to this month home. I have a better idea of how to help my people moving forward."

"That's a good thing," Nathan smiled at her. "But, for us? I want a partnership, Aurora. Where we make choices together. We might not always like the outcome, but knowing we chose a path together and can be by each other's side as we walk…errr, swim it…that's what matters most."

"It is. I can't promise I won't sometimes screw up and make poor decisions, but I can promise that I'm willing to learn and grow. With you. Nathan…" Aurora stepped back and stood before him and Nathan stood as well, a quizzical look on his face. Aurora took a deep breath and dropped to one knee.

"Aurora?" Nathan laughed down at her.

"Nathan, I love you…will you marry me?" Aurora looked up at him, confused at his laughter. He grabbed her hands and pulled her to standing again, wrapping his arms around her. "Why are you laughing at me?"

"Did you read about this in your magazines?" Nathan asked, chuckling into her hair.

"Well, yes, I did. I thought you were supposed to propose to get married."

"Technically, yes, you are meant to propose to get married. And though this is very outdated and patriarchal, typically it is the man who proposes. Not always, and I find it very refreshing that you proposed to me."

"So now I have to wait for you to propose?" Aurora pouted.

"Nope, I'm not letting you go – ever again. Yes, Aurora. I would love to marry you. Here. On Land. Anywhere and everywhere. Just don't ever leave me…okay?"

"I promise I won't. You and the babies come first, always," Aurora said and then his lips were on hers, and Aurora was so desperate for him, she almost knocked him over when she jumped him. Nathan stumbled back, catching her weight, and then lowered her to the soft grasses on the floor.

"Are we, um, private here?" Nathan asked, his eyes full of hunger for her.

"Oh yes, completely. Please, Nathan, I've missed you," Aurora was all but whimpering with need now.

"Then let me take my time with you, sweet princess. I've had a month of angsty nights dreaming over you. Now, I will exact my revenge…" Nathan said, an evil smile on his face as he traced one finger tantalizingly over the slope of her breast. It was pure torture, and Aurora glared at him.

"Did I say I wanted to marry you? I must have lost my mind. It was probably just the adrenaline of the moment… made me blabber silly things," Aurora said through narrowed eyes.

"Too late," Nathan laughed against her mouth, catching her lower lip in his and biting gently. "You're mine now."

EPILOGUE

"*I*t would have been easier to swim…" Aurora trailed off at Nathan's look. "Okay, fine, easier for *some* of us."

They'd just arrived at the Laughing Mermaid after Ezra, Irma's partner, had picked them up from Triste Island on his boat. Nothing had prepared Nathan for what fatherhood would really be like – not to mention to two Mer babies at that.

He didn't need to be putting the pilot into a panic when their babies changed mid-flight into their Mer form. Nathan still marveled at it. Who knew that Mer could change forms out of water? Aurora had explained that, yes, it was possible, but the transition was better in water. Apparently, Mer babies were so full of frenetic energy and magick that they could zip between their forms in a blink of an eye. It was a trip, that was for sure, and the whole thing still kind of blew Nathan's mind.

He caught Aurora's eyes from where she cradled Alyssa. James was curled into his arms, sleeping peacefully, though Nathan knew that peace was momentary. Much like the calm before the storm, his children had the ability to make him think he had everything under control right before they landed in some new mischief. Thinking of the calm before the storm brought Nathan back to that most horrific – and wonderful – day that still haunted his dreams some nights.

The storm that had almost cost him his life. He'd never forget the utter feeling of helplessness as waves crashed over him. Or the intense emotion that flooded him when he'd opened his eyes to see Aurora, his weeping goddess, curled over him. As highs and lows went, it was a day forever seared into his mind.

It hadn't been the last day of highs and lows for them, that was for sure. Since then, they'd had quite a roller-coaster ride for their fledgling relationship. Nathan laughed to himself. His friends had questioned how quickly he'd changed his life for this woman he'd only just met. But, after meeting Aurora, not a single one, including his mother, had ever questioned his decision again.

Aurora, quite simply, sparkled.

She won over everyone that she met – greeting them with an infectious enthusiasm and warmth – and listening wholeheartedly to their life stories. She was genuinely interested, too, not like some people who just pretend to listen while they waited for others to finish talking. Aurora was a sponge, soaking up knowledge at a dizzying speed, and she'd become a huge asset to Ezra as he worked with the ladies of the Laughing Mermaid to create an immersion course for Mer looking to explore life on land.

And then…then there'd been the day that Aurora had

finally confronted her father over her future involvement as a ruler of the village. After many late-night talks, Aurora had finally made the decision she'd been working toward for a long time. She didn't want to be the next queen. Nathan had breathed a sigh of relief, as he was certain he wasn't cut out to be the next king, by default, of the Mer. Nathan had accompanied her via her magick to the village and had watched as Aurora had plopped the twins on her father's lap and told him she was done.

King Donovan had softened since the birth of his grandchildren. He'd smiled as the twins swam circles between his legs as he tried to catch them.

"I have a proposal for you," Aurora had announced.

She'd gone on to explain, in a neat and efficient manner worthy of any corporate boardroom, why she thought a group of advisors was a stronger choice for their people, how she'd be able to help as a sitting advisor, and what that could look like for the future of their village. She also explained how much she enjoyed her work on land, how she felt she was helping the other Mer communities, and that being a mother took a lot of her time and energy as well. At that, King Donovan had laughed and nodded, still trying to catch hold of his rambunctious grandchildren.

Aurora had won her proposal and since then the king and queen had worked tirelessly alongside her and Ezra to build a ruling structure that made sense for the future of their village. So far, it had gone swimmingly. Nathan smirked at his pun, as he thought about how enthused the other Mer were with becoming more involved in their own governing.

Now, they were attending a party at the Laughing Mermaid to celebrate this new era for the Mer. Ezra and Irma had returned from a successful trip wherein they met other tribes around the world and garnered support for Ezra's United Nations of Mer plan. The launch of the Mer + Human immersion course was imminent, and Nathan couldn't have been prouder of Aurora.

And for himself, to be honest. Being with Aurora had provided him with excellent insights for his game, and he'd won several awards for the newest version. In fact, he'd been approached by not one, but two huge retailers wanting to license his designs for merchandise, and his attorneys were also reviewing an option for a movie based on his game. In some respects, his video game had become a global phenomenon and he ran it all from his little head-quarters on quiet Triste Island.

Aurora had loved the house immediately and had been thrilled with the opportunity to decorate it to her heart's content. She divided her time between land and sea, and Nathan had been able to have a lovely pool installed in record time for his children to be born in. Because, yes, that had happened faster than he'd been prepared for.

What a night…

Nothing could have prepared Nathan for his children being born under the moon in the open ocean. Even after the pool had been built, when her contractions hit – Aurora had wanted the sea. He could only go so far with her, so she'd lapped back and forth in front of their house, her mother at her side and the entire village passing by under-water to make sure she was safe. Nathan had wondered what the residents of Triste Island would do if they had known that hundreds of mermaids swam in the dark ocean just feet from the shoreline. When his children had finally been born, the ocean had lit up – just for one bright brilliant moment – and Nathan had been overcome when James, his baby boy, had swam to him immediately and curled into his arms.

Much like he was curled now.

Nathan hefted James, bigger now, but still a baby, and greeted Irma.

"GIVE HIM TO ME," Irma ordered, arms outstretched for the baby who was just waking up.

"Do as she says," Jolie warned, coming up behind him dressed in a screaming-red dress that highlighted her dark hair and hugged every inch of her curves. Her husband, Ted, a studious man with glasses like Nathan's, greeted Nathan. He liked Ted, both men sharing a natural awkwardness and a slightly perplexed air of wonderment that these magnificent creatures had chosen them to be their partners.

"He's all yours," Nathan handed James over. He had turquoise eyes, like his mother, but the dimple in his chin was all Nathan's. Nathan tapped a finger on his son's nose. "Be good for Irma."

James squealed and fist-pumped, which lead Nathan to believe that he would be a little monster.

"Don't worry, I can take care of this little imp. Now, have you seen bubbles before? Let's go look." Irma kissed the baby's cheeks and hustled over to a side table. The garden was set for a party, and though it was late – due to the nature of the event – it just made sense. Fairy lights were strung through the trees, and the tables were loaded with food and sweets. A bar held batches of specialty cocktails, and buckets of ice were filled with beers. A tent had been set up at the property next door, which Nathan had learned belonged to a mermaid named Samantha. The tent was more to block any nosy people from interrupting their party, but it also allowed the Mer to towel off and wrap the provided sarongs around their bodies.

Because that is what this was, Nathan looked around in awe. A true mingling of Mer and humans, with the Mer far outnumbering the select humans at the party. They poured from the water, naked and unabashed, toweling off and seemingly delighted in being provided with clothes to wear.

"They'd just dance naked all night if we allowed it," a voice said at his ear and Nathan turned, a grin splitting his face.

"Lola!" He hugged the café owner. "I didn't know you knew about the Mer."

"Know about them?" Lola put her hands on her hips and gave him an offended look.

"Oh, shit. You are Mer, aren't you?"

"Half. Like your darling children."

"Really?" Nathan's eyes lit. "That's...I can't believe all the people I've interacted with that had otherworldly powers."

"Oh, but don't you know? There's magick every-where," Lola grinned, squeezing his arm and tugging him forward. "Let me introduce you."

Nathan quickly sought out Aurora, who gave him a go-

ahead look when he raised an eyebrow in question. She
was happy speaking to Mirra who had Alyssa hanging on
her shoulder and poking at the tattoos on the arm of
Mirra's husband, Silas.

"This is Prince. He's human, like you, but he's always
been an ally of the Mer. Smartest man on Siren Island,"
Lola said, introducing Nathan to a dark-skinned man with
a smile that lit his whole face.

"Now 'dis 'ere man 'de one who make 'de mermaid
game?" Prince sized up Nathan.

"Yes, sir. That's me."

"It's a good game, 'dat's 'de truth of it. But I've got
some suggestions." Prince pulled Nathan close. To his
amazement, the man's suggestions were so good that soon
Nathan was requesting his contact info so he could discuss
collaborating with him. Prince pulled a sleek phone from
his weathered shorts pocket and surprised him with a QR
code for his contact info. Apparently, QR codes were
making a comeback and Nathan made a note to add those
to his game packaging.

He spoke with Avery and Roman, a couple who met
filming a reality show, and exchanged contact information
to talk about the movie business and why he should think
twice over the movie option currently sitting on his attor-
ney's desk. Samantha and Lucas, the neighbors, immediately invited him over for brunch the next day when they
had found Nathan surrounded by the group of dogs that
seemed to belong to nobody and everybody at once. He'd
always wanted a dog, and he'd caught Aurora laughing at
him across the garden with a knowing look in her eyes.

Gage, Lola's husband, talked boats with Silas, and both

men's eyes had gleamed with interest when they learned Nathan was the video game guy. Here, he'd thought he'd always be the awkward nerd who would forever be horrible at socializing and fitting in with others. Who knew that being a video game geek would turn out to be such an asset later in life? But in reality, Nathan no longer felt the same awkwardness he'd once carried around like a shield.

Because now he'd found his people, Nathan realized, looking around at the magickal mix of Mer and oddball humans, dancing under the fairy lights and drinking fruity cocktails with paper umbrellas tucked in the glasses.

"Hey, handsome," Aurora said, wrapping an arm around his waist. He smiled down at her, so incredibly grateful that he'd taken the beach route home that one evening that had forever changed his life. This stunning, huge-hearted woman was his. If ever there was a miracle, it was her, and Nathan's heart swelled with love. "I think my father wants to make a speech. But after that...while we have free childcare...I was thinking..." Aurora leaned up and whispered a dirty suggestion in Nathan's ear that had his cheeks pinkening.

"Um, yes," Nathan cleared his throat. "I'd very much like that."

"I thought so," Aurora purred, and Nathan did his best to think clean thoughts when Aurora's father stood, a sarong wrapped around his waist, and raised his hands for attention. The music stopped and the party quieted.

"My good people, both Mer and human alike, I welcome you here today in a first event of its kind," King Donovan smiled at the crowd. "We hope for more in the future, in a controlled and safe way."

The crowd clapped in appreciation.

"I'd like to thank Ezra and Irma for hosting us, and for the good work they are doing to unite not only our tribes of the world, but in making headway in forming a safe alliance with vetted humans. This will go a long way toward protecting our people, and the oceans we live in. As you know, the oceans are threatened, and without healthy oceans, neither of our people will survive. Together, with concentrated effort and good will, I can see us making a difference."

More cheers sounded, and Aurora squeezed Nathan's waist.

"Finally, I'd like to give special recognition to my daughter and her husband, Nathan. Not only have you provided us with the best grandchildren a man could hope for, but you've done something even better – you've given hope to not only our people, but to an old Mer as well. You see, I was stubborn for a very long time. Set in my ways. I thought I knew what was best for my people, and nobody could tell me different. It took my beautiful and talented daughter, and her endless thirst for knowledge, running away from home for me to see the truth. And the truth is no one person is one hundred percent right. The future lies with those who refuse to be blind, and instead lift their faces to the sun. I'm proud of you, Aurora, for being the change that I was too blind to see. You bring honor to our people."

Aurora's eyes filled and then she was across the garden, hugging her father, while Nathan looked on, pride filling his heart.

It was a new day for the Mer, and much like the Oracle

had predicted, Aurora had been the changemaker for her people.

ARE you looking for more magickal romance? Hop over to the rocky shores of Ireland where the elemental fae learn that love is fated.

Song of the Fae - Available now!

SONG OF THE FAE

The man beckoned to her from beneath the silky surface of the sea. The familiar unease unfurled in Imogen's core, and instead of turning away as she usually did, Imogen met his gaze and tried to study him objectively.

The man's grin widened. He was really more of a creature, she supposed. His skin was so white that the pearlescent sheen of it gleamed in the soft light from the moon, reminding Imogen of the underbelly of a salmon. Eyes of milky opalescence blinked at her, flashes of pinks and greens shimmering in their depths. Both beautiful and terrifying, Imogen swallowed against her suddenly dry throat as the man raised a hand and beckoned to her once more. The most surprising thing? A part of her wanted to follow him. To dive into the wintry cold sea, sinking into the inky depths, and deliver her mind over to the delusions that had danced on the edge of her consciousness for years now. When that urge became dangerously close to engulfing her, Imogen turned from the bow of the boat and shuddered, gulping in a few deep breaths and forcing herself to break the pull she felt from the creature in the water.

That she'd seen most of her life, that is. In her dreams as well.

It was always the same man who followed her – slipping silently just below the ocean's surface – during stormy nights or calm blue-sky days. A part of her hated this creature, for his appearance threw her own sanity into question, and yet another part of her yearned to go to him. It was as though he was a missing link in her life, but Imogen didn't have the time or inclination to dissect just what he symbolized for her. Maybe, someday, when her boat was paid off and she could take a moment to breathe, Imogen would plop herself down on a therapist's couch and pour out all of her fears. But that day had not yet come, and Imogen doubted it ever would. The luxury of analysis and self-improvement was not afforded to a person like her, who spent every waking moment trying to build her business and keep her deck crew employed.

Annoyed with herself, and the direction of her thoughts, Imogen strode across the deck of the *Mystic Pirate*, her very own charter boat, and locked the wheelhouse. They'd arrived in Grace's Cove that morning, the harbor hugged by rolling green hills with colorful houses dotting the winding streets. It was a charming village, and Imogen had been scouting for longer charter trips for the American tourists that visited each summer. She wanted to meet with a few B&B owners to see about offering a land and sea package holiday. Imogen's instincts told her that a package that mixed the best of what Ireland had to offer would be well-received, particularly by tourists who had limited vacation days.

Imogen leapt onto the dock, pausing to slip on her shoes, and then walked toward the village, still feeling the familiar rocking of the boat beneath her. It was always that way when she stepped onto land, Imogen thought with a bemused smile on her face. At sea, she was most stable, while on land she felt off-kilter and out of sorts. With no family to speak of, and very few friends, the gentle rocking motion that plagued most sailors when they went to land was a comfortable reminder to Imogen of where she really belonged.

A captain of her own ship, controlling her own destiny on the water that she loved. *Her home.*

She'd never fit in the regular world anyway, for she had no frame of reference for how the usual things were done. She'd never had birthday parties or played sports and had just enough schooling to get by. No, Imogen wasn't going to bake a pie with a baby perched on her hip. The very thought made her laugh, as the vision of that life seemed more delusional to her than the creature that followed her at the ocean's edge.

A recent rain had left puddles in the streets of Grace's Cove, and they reflected the lights of the shops and restaurants that clustered together, winding up the street toward the top of the hill. Imogen strolled along, her hands in the pockets of her fleece jacket, and hummed a song that had been niggling at her brain for a while. It was one of those things where she just couldn't place the tune, and it had been driving her wild for months. She heard the song in her dreams, and she caught herself singing it during the day while she helped to clean the boat or tallied their provisions. It was a melancholy tune, almost heartbreaking in its need, and Imogen still hadn't been able to discover where she'd learned of it.

Opal eyes blinked at her from a puddle on the street and Imogen skidded to a stop, her stomach twisting, as the creature from the ocean smiled up at her. *This was...this was new.* Sweat broke out across her brow. Fear gripped her and she turned to run, only to slam directly into a wall.

Well, at least what felt like a wall. Hands gripped her arms, steadying her, and Imogen's breath caught as her gaze rose from the buttons of a flannel shirt and up, up, up to the face of a glowering man. Stormy gray eyes, a rough beard, and a chiseled jawline would be enough to make any woman swoon.

For Imogen, it was like a plug finding a socket, and strange energy coursed through her, making her feel both alive and inconceivably resilient.

I want to kiss him.

The thought shocked her enough to step back, cutting their physical contact, and the hum of energy lessened... but it did not entirely abate. Imogen was not a lusty person, oh no, if anything she found sex to be tedious or boring most times. Which is why it had been ages since she'd let a man touch her. And yet now, it was like all her senses woke up and she wanted, well, things she shouldn't want from a stranger who was glaring at her on the street.

"What was that song you were singing?" The man's voice, like honey spilled on gravel, caused her insides to go liquid so she just stared at him in confusion for a moment until his words registered. *What an odd thing to ask.* Heat crept up her cheeks when she realized she was just standing there with her mouth hanging open like a fish out of water.

"Um, sure and it's just a made-up tune, really. A bit of nonsense at that." Imogen cleared her throat and took another step back. *This man was so intense.*

"Is it?" The man's brow furrowed, and he seemed to be considering his next words carefully. Imogen wondered if she should take this opportunity to flee, but the confusing mix of feelings that toiled inside her kept her rooted to the spot. A door from the restaurant behind her swung open, and a patron stepped onto the street. Laughter, music, the clinking of silverware, along with the delicious scent of garlic danced in the air, and Imogen was grateful that she wasn't alone on the street with this stranger. A man easily double her size, built of muscle, with a storm cloud of emotions on his handsome face.

"I believe it to be, yes." Imogen spoke her words carefully, taking another step away, though her body urged her to step forward and back into his arms. It had felt safe there, though why Imogen needed to feel safe, she couldn't be certain. Her mind flashed back to the creature in the puddle. Okay, sure, maybe a big strapping man by her side wasn't a bad thing. Maybe just not *this* man…

"What are you?" His tone was clipped, and Imogen's eyes widened when he clenched his fists at his sides.

"Surely, you've seen a female before, haven't you then?" Imogen arched a brow at the man. She rocked lightly back on her heels, her hand going to her waistband where her favorite knife was tucked. Imogen had learned a lot working the docks, and protecting herself had been at the top of the list.

"You heard my question." The man glanced to the sky, his worry flashing across his face as lightning exploded in the velvety darkness.

There were no storm clouds.

Imogen swallowed, worry filling her, as the man's eyes sought hers once more.

"And I answered it." Imogen lifted her chin.

"Something's wrong." The man moved to brush past her, but stopped just at her side, and looked down at her. "Be careful with your songs, little one. You don't know what you're doing."

"Excuse me?" Imogen whirled as the man raced up the street, preternaturally quiet. Unease slipped through her at the faint purple tinge glowing in a soft silhouette around the man. It wasn't the first time she'd seen such a thing, but it was something she decidedly tried to ignore. Much like the faces in the water, Imogen wasn't interested in trying to explain why she could see people's auras. At least that's what her research had led her to believe. One big problem? From what she'd learned, auras came in all colors.

Imogen could only see *two* aura colors. Silver and purple. Neither of which helped convince herself that she was, indeed, normal.

While a pint and a bit of home-cooked food had initially been what had drawn Imogen from the *Mystic Pirate* and into the village, now she turned abruptly and made her way back to her boat, hurrying as another bolt of lightning lanced across the night sky.

Whatever problems plagued Grace's Cove were not her own, Imogen decided, breathing out a sigh of relief when she stepped back onto her ship. Unlocking the door to her wheelhouse, she slipped inside and locked the door behind her, and then clambered down a short flight of stairs that led to the galley and lounge area. She crossed the gleaming wood floor and opened a cabinet to pull out a bottle of Green Spot which was usually reserved for the guests and poured herself a healthy glass. Leaning against the counter, Imogen took a sip, and the familiar heat of whiskey soothed her throat.

What are you?

The man's words drifted back to her.

"I wish I knew," Imogen said out loud, before lifting her glass in a silent toast to the strangely glowing man she'd met on the street. "Trust me, sir, I wish I knew."

Song of the Fae - Available now!

AFTERWORD

Thank you, my friends, for joining me on this delightful journey to Siren Island. It's been so lovely to share my love for the ocean with you all. As many of you know, I spend much of my time underwater photographing sea life, and I'm constantly astounded by the beauty and complexity that the ocean has to offer. There is still so much that is undiscovered and unexplored in her depths, I can't help that hope mermaids are real. Maybe, one day, I'll catch a glimpse of one on my night dives.

In the meantime, we can all work together to create healthy and happy oceans. For those who reach out to me with questions regarding organizations that support our oceans, below are some of my favorites:

Coral Restoration Foundation

Sea Shepherd Conservation Society

Mission Blue Organization

Project AWARE

Shark Alliance

Other ways you can assist in helping our oceans?

Please don't contribute to the hatred of sharks. Our oceans need them for a healthy eco-system and the sea is their home. Remember, it is never shark-infested waters - they live there. Next up, you can look at reducing your plastic consumption and focus on reusable products. There's also many lovely reef-safe sunscreens that you can use for when you do go in the sea that are less harmful to the reefs.

Thanks for caring about our oceans - every little bit helps!

If you would like to see some beautiful photos of my Scuba diving adventures then good news! I have a free download called 'Mermaid View' on the freebie page of my website.

www.triciaomalley.com/free

Love,

Tricia

THE WILDSONG SERIES

ALSO BY TRICIA O'MALLEY

Song of the Fae

Melody of Flame

Chorus of Ashes

"The magic of Fae is so believable. I read these books in one sitting and can't wait for the next one. These are books you will reread many times."

- Amazon Review

Available in audio, e-book & paperback!

Available Now

THE ISLE OF DESTINY SERIES

ALSO BY TRICIA O'MALLEY

Stone Song

Sword Song

Spear Song

Sphere Song

A completed series.

Available in audio, e-book & paperback!

"Love this series. I will read this multiple times. Keeps you on the edge of your seat. It has action, excitement and romance all in one series."

- Amazon Review

THE MYSTIC COVE SERIES

Wild Irish Heart

Wild Irish Eyes

Wild Irish Soul

Wild Irish Rebel

Wild Irish Roots: Margaret & Sean

Wild Irish Witch

Wild Irish Grace

Wild Irish Dreamer

Wild Irish Christmas (Novella)

Wild Irish Sage

Wild Irish Renegade

Wild Irish Moon

"I have read thousands of books and a fair percentage have been romances. Until I read Wild Irish Heart, I never had a book actually make me believe in love."- Amazon Review

Available in audio, e-book & paperback!

CONTACT ME

I hope my books have added a little magick into your life. If you have a moment to add some to my day, you can help by telling your friends and leaving a review. Word-of-mouth is the most powerful way to share my stories. Thank you.

Love books? What about fun giveaways? Nope? Okay, can I entice you with underwater photos and cute dogs? Let's stay friends, receive my emails and contact me by signing up at my website

www.triciaomalley.com

Or find me on Facebook and Instagram.
@triciaomalleyauthor

Author's Acknowledgement

A very deep and heartfelt *thank you* goes to those in my life who have continued to support me on this wonderful journey of being an author. At times, this job can be very stressful, however, I'm grateful to have the sounding board of my friends who help me through the trickier moments of self-doubt. An extra-special thanks goes to The Scotsman, who is my number one supporter and always manages to make me smile.

Please know that every book I write is a part of me, and I hope you feel the love that I put into my stories. Without my readers, my work means nothing, and I am grateful that you all are willing to share your valuable time with the worlds I create. I hope each book brings a smile to your face and for just a moment it gives you a much-needed escape.

Slainté, Tricia O'Malley